fox

Matthew Sweeney

BLOOMSBURY
CHILDREN'S
BOOKS

First published in Great Britain in 2002 by Bloomsbury Publishing Plc
38 Soho Square, London, W1D 3HB

Copyright © by Matthew Sweeney 2002
The moral right of the author has been asserted

A CIP catalogue record of this book is available from the British Library
ISBN 0 7475 6040 4

Printed in Great Britain by Clays Ltd, St Ives plc

10 9 8 7 6 5 4 3 2 1

fox

dedication

foreword

It has been over 5 years since a series of events came together that have led to the publication of this book. It began when I became a volunteer for the Cork Simon Community in late 1995. On Christmas Eve I was introduced to the soup run, a year round project that provides soup, dinners, blankets and companionship to those in Cork City who are sleeping rough on the streets or living in substandard conditions.

It was at this time that I first met James. He lived in a caravan on a busy road surrounded by the many 'treasures' he had collected from the local dump. His way of life, his appearance, and his eccentricities often scared people who came in contact with him. However, this did not seem to be the case where children were concerned. One day in the play school where I was teaching, I overheard a parent trying to discipline her child by saying that if he didn't behave she would take him to James' caravan and leave him. To this the child eagerly replied, 'Can we go there now?' He was delighted at the prospect of spending time with James.

From this simple encounter an idea arose to write a children's book. I contacted a friend of mine, Damhnait Sweeney, who had worked with me on the *Cork Cookbook*. She mentioned that her brother, Matthew, was a children's writer. After I saw some of his work, I knew he would be ideal for the project and happily he agreed to write the story. We were then fortunate enough to secure funding from the Loyola Foundation of Washington, D.C. and I am very grateful to them. I am also indebted to Patrick O'Brien who has worked so diligently on the marketing and to Martin Faherty for his support.

In the time it has taken to bring this book to fruition, many of the homeless men and women I had the privilege to work with have since died. However, they have left me a tremendous legacy. Most of the meaningful lessons I have learned in my lifetime have evolved from knowing residents of the Simon Community. The homeless have taught me how to hope in desperation; how to help others, even if I have nothing myself; how to maintain a sense of humour in the midst of misery; how to hold onto simple dreams when everything seems impossible, and how to be individual in a world dicated by convention and routine.

I will forever be indebted to those I have known. I see this book as a testament to all the homeless who have struggled and died on the city streets. It is a tribute to who they are, how they live, and what they mean in this world. I hope they will not be forgotten.

Ann McCarthy-Farrell

the fox

The day after I moved to the city I saw the fox. I was on my bike exploring the streets round our new home and there he was, staring at me. I braked and put one foot on the ground. He was wrapped round the neck of a man, his red brush of a tail hanging down one side, his little head with its bright eyes on the other side. And the eyes were watching me – he was a living scarf!

I looked at the man then. He had long red hair and a red beard. The red matched the fox's red. I wondered if that was why the fox had picked the man. Or had the man picked the fox? But you never hear of foxes being pets.

The man was sitting on the ground, in a doorway, with a blanket wrapped round him. In front of him was a red beret with some coins in it. Not too many, I could see. I had no money with me to put in the beret. The man stared at me and the fox stared at me, and they made no sound or movement. I wondered if they sat there all day. And where did they sleep? What did they eat? Where did they go to the toilet?

I decided to go on. It's never nice being stared at, even if these stares were not unfriendly. I had one last big look at the two of them, because I wanted to remember them clearly and draw them when I got home. It would be the first drawing I'd do in the city, and I wanted it to be a good one. I hurried away.

the drawing

As soon as I had my dinner I went upstairs. I got my drawing notebook out and my pencil, and I closed my eyes to get the picture of the man and the fox back in my head. Drawing was what I liked to do best, and I was good at it. I wanted to be a painter when I grew up, and have my paintings in art galleries and museums for people to go and look at them.

I started with the man, as I'd drawn men before, and beards were easy to do. The fox was new for me – I don't think I'd seen one before, except in photographs. But I did well enough. I got a red pencil and coloured in the fox, and the man's hair and beard. I didn't use colours usually – and I put no other colour in the drawing – but there was so much red in what I'd seen that I had to use it.

I took it down to show my mum. She was drinking wine and watching the telly. My dad was checking the pubs out, to find one he liked, but he never took any interest in my drawings anyway. Mum did, a bit.

She didn't like this one much, though. Didn't find it believable.

'A fox wouldn't wrap itself round someone's neck like that,' she said. 'And you don't find foxes in cities.'

'You do,' I said. 'I'll bring you to this one.'

'You will not,' she said. 'I'm watching this programme. Anyway, I don't want you going near people who live on the streets. You don't know what you might catch from them.'

second sighting

Next morning I was up early and out on my bike again. No guesses for where I headed – but the two of them weren't there! I pedalled fast up the street in my disappointment, nearly knocking down a lady pushing a pram across the road. Then I slowed down, thinking that not everybody liked to get up early. I knew nothing about the sleeping patterns of foxes.

I decided to hang around, waiting to see if they'd show up. I did a loose tour of the neighbouring streets, always coming back to the street where I'd met the fox. I passed several other men sitting in doorways, or still sleeping there, wrapped up in cardboard boxes. Normally I wouldn't have looked twice at them, but today I slowed down and stared at each of them. Who knew in what way they might be interesting? None of them had a fox, that was sure, but they might have something else that was different. Being out here on the streets was different, wasn't it? Most people lived in houses. I liked people who were different. My mum's and dad's friends bored me.

I went into a park that I found at the bottom of a street. People were already out walking their dogs. I'd wanted a dog. In fact, I'd pestered my mum and dad to get me a dog for my tenth birthday recently, but they wouldn't. They got me a camera instead! Now, all the dogs I saw looked ugly compared to the fox. A fox was like a dog, too, only cuter, but I couldn't very well ask my parents for a fox.

I headed back to the street, but just as I was turning in, I saw the two I was looking for in front of me. I slowed right down, staying behind them as they walked along. They weren't fast. The man walked with a limp, and he was helped by a black stick. He was wearing the red beret and a heavy brown coat. The fox trotted along beside him. There was no lead, and no need for one either – the fox stayed only a foot or two away from the man. People walk-ing by stopped and stared at the fox, but the man ignored them. Once a big dog started barking and growling and the fox looked anx-ious, but the man threatened it with his stick and its owner dragged it away.

When they got to the doorway they'd been in yesterday, they sat down. The man lifted the fox to his neck, and laid the beret upside-down in front of him. I noticed that it was the door-way of an empty shop, with a For Sale sign on the window. By now I was right beside them, exchanging stares again. The fox seemed to recognise me. I reached in my pocket and took out fifty pence from my pocket-money which I'd brought to throw in the beret. It was the first coin in there – maybe it would attract more. The man raised his finger to his right eyebrow and gave the faintest of smiles. Was it a smile, at all? It was hard to be sure.

At any rate, I'd seen enough. I headed home to draw the pair of them walking up the street.

the new school

The next day was Sunday, and wet, and the man and the fox didn't show. Or at least, they weren't in their usual doorway when I cycled there to check. My mother was annoyed with me for going out in the rain, so I didn't try a again. I had a feeling they wouldn't be there. I wondered what they'd be doing instead.

I spent the day reading about foxes in an animal encyclopedia I'd got two Christmases before, copying the pictures of foxes that I saw there. I imagined the curious barking noises they make and wanted to hear the man's fox bark. I read about white arctic foxes up in the Arctic Circle. I annoyed my parents' heads talking to them about foxes. My father was listening to rock music and shouted at me to go away. My mother was doing the ironing and

11

day dreaming. I went upstairs again.

Next morning was Monday, and the first day at my new school. I hated going there, where I'd know nobody. I hadn't much liked my last school either. It was in the town we'd just moved from, a hundred miles away. I'd kept getting into trouble. Kids had kept picking on me, teachers had kept picking on me. I'd lost my temper sometimes and struck out at people. Once I'd kicked a teacher who'd slapped me – I'd had to stay home for a week after that, and my dad had grounded me for a month, and made me write a letter of apology. The worst thing I'd done – and it had been half an accident – was smash the glass front door one day when my mum was late to collect me. I hadn't liked anything we'd done in class, either – except drawing, and poetry writing the day the poet had come in to work with us.

My mum said this school would be different. She talked about a fresh start. But she didn't tell me all the kids would laugh at my accent, and imitate it. Two girls ran after me through the playground, mocking me.

Country boy, they called me, singing a made-up song. One boy tripped me as I tried to escape the girls. I lay there on the ground as the whole playground laughed at me, till a teacher came over, lifted me up and took me into the empty classroom.

'This is only because you're a new boy,' she said. 'They'll soon get used to you, and you'll make friends.'

I doubted it, but I said nothing. I wished I was back in my bedroom.

on the streets

I wanted to cheer myself up by seeing the man and the fox again on my way home, but I didn't want my mother to see them – even if it did prove my first drawing was true. Anyway, I didn't think she'd appreciate the detour. It was a long enough walk – much longer than the walk from the school in our old town had been. Cities were impossibly big places. If I rode around on my bike all day, every day, for a month I still wouldn't get round the whole of this one. And I'd surely end up completely lost, and joining the people who lived on the streets.

I tried to imagine what that would be like, and couldn't. How could they stand being outside, with people staring at them all the time? Or worse still, ignoring them, as if they were lamp posts. They couldn't get any privacy at all.

I knew how good it was to close the door of my room when I needed to. I could do what I wanted in there. And what did they do when it rained hard, or got really cold? And didn't bad people coming out of the pubs sometimes try to kick them to death, when they staggered past them lying in doorways there?

Of course, I didn't know if the man and the fox slept in that doorway. I didn't think so; they had no sleeping bags or cardboard boxes with them. And hadn't I seen them walking along the street towards their doorway? That meant they were coming from somewhere. I decided there and then that as soon as possible I would find out where they lived.

the black stick

The next time I saw the two it was Saturday – almost a whole week later! It had been a bad week, but nothing had been as bad as that first day. Most of the kids had begun to leave me alone, and I was trying hard not to react to the rest. At least the teacher was nice enough, and had praised my drawing. That was on the second day. I told my mum on the way home and she suggested I bring in some of the drawings I'd done in my room. I was surprised to hear this, as I didn't think Mum took that much interest in them, but next day I showed my teacher the two drawings I'd done of the man and the fox. She was very taken with them, and showed them to the class. She said I should do more.

The next drawing I decided to do was of the

man's black stick. I had to take a good look at it first, so I cycled over to the shop doorway. I got off my bike and stood in front of the man and the fox. They knew who I was by now. I was glad to see a few banknotes among the coins in the beret. I said hello, and the man nodded. The fox had his eyes on me. I wanted him to wag his tail a little, but he didn't. I didn't know if foxes wagged their tails.

I pointed to the stick which was lying on the ground and asked the man if I could hold it for a minute. He took his time but eventually he nodded, reached down and handed the stick to me, handle first. I took it in my hands. It was heavy, made of smooth black wood. The head was carved to look like a skull. It looked African. It must have taken hours to make.

I handed it back, and thanked the man. He nodded again, then surprised me by speaking.

'What's your name?' he asked. His voice was a rumble from far inside him, as if he didn't use it much and had to dredge it up from his innards.

'G-G-Gerard,' I said. 'Gerard Lavelle.'

'Good,' said the man, as if I'd given the right answer, which of course, as it was my real name, I had done. It just didn't seem an answer that would make someone say 'good'.

I waited for him to say more but there was no more coming. I wanted to ask *him* questions – ask him about the fox, about where they lived, about why he was here on the street, but I couldn't. Not yet. I felt awkward now, standing there, so with a last look at the black stick, I said goodbye to the two of them, and got on my bike again. All the way home I was excited that we'd spoken. It hadn't been much, but it was a start. I felt silly I hadn't at least asked him his name after I'd told him mine, but I could do that the next time I saw them. Did the fox have a name? I'd ask that, too. I bet he did.

I tried drawing the black stick straight away but I couldn't get it right. The head wasn't anything like a skull in my drawing. But that night I dreamed of the stick floating in the air, turning round like someone had twirled it and flung it high, and it had stayed there, weightless, in slow motion. Every now and then I got a good close-up of the head, and when I woke the next morning I tried the drawing again and there, in my notebook, appeared the black stick.

his son

I didn't leave it so long next time. I managed to slip out of the house again, shortly after I returned from a bearable day at school. My dad was out, at his new job, and my mum was distracted, watching one of her soap operas. She was making the most of the time before she started her new job at the hospital.

I didn't know what time the man and the fox left the doorway and went to wherever they lived, but I figured they wouldn't be gone yet. I was right. There they were in their doorway. I could see them both picking me out as I neared them.

'It's Mr Lavelle, come to visit us again,' said the man. The fox looked at him as he spoke. I dismounted, left the bike lying on the pavement, and crouched on my hunkers in front of them. They'd picked a quiet street that didn't have too much traffic, although plenty of pedestrians passed along. Pretty canny, I thought.

'Hello,' I said. 'What are your names? I've told you mine.'

The man laughed.

'I forgot my name a long time ago, but if you need something to call me, Clint will do. And this fellow here' – He turned to look into the fox's eyes. 'He mightn't look like it, but he's my son.'

'Your son?' I asked, disbelievingly.

The man threw his head back and laughed again.

'Not literally, young Gerard,' he said. 'But good as, good as. I call him Russ.'

The fox looked at him again, and I thought I saw the big tail wag slightly. I remembered all the questions I wanted to ask the man, but a completely different question came out.

'Does Russ bark?' I asked.

'Does Russ bark? Does a dog-fox bark? Here, let me show you.'

He lifted the fox from his shoulders and put him standing on the ground. He himself sat up straight, and in a loud whisper, said twice the word *Rats!* At that the fox started turning his head from side to side, and letting small high-pitched barks out of him. The man laughed, lifted the fox to his chest, and said into his ear, 'No rats here, Russ, no rats.'

Then the fox was back round his neck as before, placid as usual.

I decided to be bold now.

'Where do you and Russ live?'

'Oh, not far from here, not far, at all. We might be near neighbours of yours. I don't think you live in our street, though.'

He laughed his head off at this, and I didn't get the joke. I thought about what he'd said about his name, but I didn't think he was Clint, so I couldn't call him that.

'Will you bring me there, where you live?' I asked him.

'I don't think your parents would like that,' he said.

'What are you really called? I don't believe

you're Clint.'

'I told you I don't remember, young Gerard. Run along home now. Your parents will be wondering where you are.'

So grumpily I got back on my bike and pedalled away.

the huff

I was annoyed with the man after that. He could have answered me straight. Telling me he was called Clint, telling me the fox was his son! So I avoided them for the rest of the week.

I let my annoyance show at school, too, by picking a fight with one of the boys who was still bugging me. I won the fight, but I was still sorry I started it. It got some of the kids who'd started to accept me back against me. And one of the teachers who'd been nice to me saw the fight and was less friendly to me afterwards.

And I couldn't draw at all. Tried to, but wasn't in the mood, and the results were awful. I ripped the pages out and flushed them down the toilet.

One thing that had stuck in my head from that last meeting with the man and the fox was the fox reacting to the word *Rats!* Did foxes eat rats? All the books I read described them breaking into henhouses and eating chickens, or ducks, or geese. I remembered a song my grandfather used to sing about a fox breaking into a farm, when the farmer was away on the town-o, and gorging himself on all the goslings. But then, as the week went on, I asked myself how many chickens, ducks or geese would be found in a city? This fox was a city fox. He had to live. There were plenty of rats in a city.

I wondered, too, about the man telling me the fox was his son. Did he have a son that he didn't see any more? I didn't always get on with my dad but I was glad he was there. That got me thinking that the man – who might be named Clint or not – had not been horrible to me. He'd been joking with me, playing. At least he'd remembered my name from the one time I'd told him. So many of my parents' friends could never remember my name. And they would never talk to me either. I might as well be a dog sitting in the room when they came to visit.

Or a fox. It occurred to me then that although I might have been annoyed with the man, I'd never been annoyed with the fox, and it was the fox I'd noticed first. And I did believe *he* was called Russ. So I resolved, as soon as I could, to go back and visit them again, and say nothing about why I'd stayed away.

the present

To make up for staying away, I decided to bring the man and the fox a present. I brought them my first drawing of the two of them. I got an old frame and put the drawing in it. I was a bit sorry to be giving the drawing away, as I liked it, but I could always draw it again.

I put it in the pannier of my bicycle and rode slowly, with constant looks backwards to make sure it didn't fall out, until I came to the red-haired duo. The man raised his eyebrows as far as they could go.

'Look who's back,' he said, so loudly and slowly that people turned to stare. I ignored this and handed him the drawing.

'I've brought you a present,' I said.

'Oh, the young Jack Yeats,' he said, laughing.

But he took the drawing and looked at it carefully, turning it in the light. He thrust it under the fox's nose, so he could have a look at it, too. Then he nodded and propped it up against the door jamb.

'Thank you,' he said, 'we've never been drawn before. Photographs, yes, but no drawings. I've always preferred drawings.'

I nodded at this, thinking of my camera, and of how I'd barely used it yet. I'd thought of bringing it out and photographing the man and the fox but I was now glad I hadn't done so. I looked at the drawing sitting there, then up at the man and the fox, and I felt pleased I'd brought the drawing.

I sat cross-legged on the ground in front of them. Some people were giving me funny looks, and one woman was clearly disgusted, but I didn't care. It was a sunny autumn day and I was with my friends.

And there were questions I wanted to ask, so I jumped straight in.

'Where are you from? And what's really your name?'

The man laughed at this.

'I told you I lost my name a long time ago. I've no use for it any more. People know me – when they know me at all – as the man with the fox. I've spoken more to you than to anyone in years. I speak to the fox, of course, but he has no need for my name. And I forget where I'm from, too. And why is that, young Gerard? Because for many more years than you've been on this earth I sailed the seas.'

'You were a sailor?'

'Ah, that I was!'

'Where did you sail to, then?'

'I sailed everywhere – Africa, Japan, Greenland. Round the Cape of Good Hope. Calcutta and the coast of Malibar, Gibraltar, Tierra del Fuego, Van Diemen's Land. Down the Suez Canal. Sicily and Cyprus. There isn't anywhere I haven't been.

'Wow!' I said. 'You've been to all those places? Did Russ go with you?'

'I didn't know the fox then.'

I looked at the man sitting in the doorway, and thought of him criss-crossing the seas.

'If you went everywhere, I said, then why are you here?'

'That was then,' he said. 'It's all done with. Now is here.'

For me, who'd never been out of Ireland, there didn't seem any doubt which time in his life I'd prefer. But he didn't have the fox then.

With the fox snug on his shoulder, the man didn't look sad at all that he wasn't on the seas. I thanked him for telling me all that, said good-bye, and cycled home.

the fight

The day afterwards, I was still thinking of what the man had said as I walked to school. I was walking there on my own now, since my mum had started at the hospital. Imagine travelling so much! I really wanted to travel when I got older. Maybe this year, with my mum and dad in new jobs, we'd go abroad for a holiday. I fancied Africa. I'd looked in an atlas the night before at the places the man had gone to, and I'd checked some of them out in an encyclopedia. Africa looked the best.

This kind of thinking didn't prepare me at all for the ambush at the school gates. A boy jumped out from behind a tree and started punching me. He was one of the boys who still kept saying things to me, and now he was taunting me for being an artist.

'Think you're great, don't you, for doing those drawings? Only girls draw.'

A couple of other boys, his usual cronies, joined in the mocking, but they left the punching to him. The way he was going about it, he needed no help.

But if there was one thing I'd learned in my previous school it was how to look after myself. So I laid into him as hard as I could, and soon it was he who was in trouble. I didn't just use my fists, either, but I kicked as well.

'Hey!' he shouted. 'Stop fighting dirty.'

'Who started the fight?' I shouted back. 'I didn't want to fight at all.'

By now a crowd of noisy kids had surrounded us, and I had the boy on the ground, thumping him. We were both a bit bloodied by this stage. I hit him one last time, then got to my feet, glaring at his cronies, just in time to see the Headteacher himself swing round the gate with a stony face.

He brought us both into his office and shouted at us for letting the school and ourselves down. He gave me a particularly hard time because I was a new boy, and because he'd seen me emerge triumphant from the fight. I tried to tell him I hadn't started it, and was only defending myself, but he wasn't interested. He told us both to stay out of school for a week, gave us letters to take to our parents, and said if there was a repeat of this we'd be expelled.

I was glad he hadn't seen last week's fight, and hoped the teacher who had seen it wouldn't tell. I *had* started that one, but it had been provoked. OK, I'd been in a bad mood, but if the boy hadn't been horrible to me I wouldn't have hit him. The same old story was happening again at this school. School and I didn't seem to get on!

gaol

I was sentenced by my father to gaol for that
week. The gaol was our house – I was not to
set foot out of it. He'd wanted to lock me in my
room but my mother hadn't allowed him to.
They'd had a shouting match in front of me
about it, but my mother had said I was her son,
too, and what my father wanted to do was inhu-
man. She threw all her objections at him – how
would I go to the toilet? what would I do for
food? what would happen if the house went on
fire? – and gradually wore him down.

Despite this defence, she was just as annoyed
with me as he was, and completely agreed that I
shouldn't be allowed to leave the house. I knew
there was one problem in their enforcing this,
however – the front door had only a yale lock
and could always be opened from the inside.

They did confiscate my key, so that if I did find myself outside, and the door happened to close, I would be trapped there until the first of them arrived home to find me. As if I would let something like that happen!

So that first morning the two of them went off to work and left me in an unlocked gaol without a gaoler. I was there when they left – they made sure to get me up before they went – and I was still there when they got home. But I didn't stay there all day.

What I was supposed to do, according to my mother, was work hard at all aspects of my schoolwork. This was a week to turn everything around, she said, so I could go back to school with a completely different attitude that would amaze the teachers. As if it was that easy!

I did some schoolwork, of course – my mother would check up on me in the evening – and I stayed in most of the time, but I did slip out. I was very careful about it. It wasn't too early or too late in the day, too near to the time they'd left, or might return – my dad was quite capable of lurking around a corner for half an hour or so, sticking his head out from time to time to see if he could catch me. I often thought he should have been a policeman. I made sure no one was looking when I left the house or slipped back in. The fact that we were new and living in a city helped me here, as my parents knew none of the neighbours yet, and could not depend on any of them to act as spies. I left the snib on the door so that although it looked closed I could push it open again. This was a bit risky, as regards burglars, but I figured if a burglar wanted to rob the house, he'd find a way of getting in. Anyway, I wasn't going to be gone for very long.

The man and the fox were surprised to see me.

'Why aren't you at school?' the man asked.

'I'm suspended for a week,' I said. 'For fighting.'

I expected the man to like that, but he didn't.

'Fighting? That's not good, at all, Gerard Lavelle. Fighting gets you nowhere. And it's not good being out of school for a week.'

'You didn't need school to become a sailor,'

I said.

'Oh, yes I did. I needed geography to know where I was going. I needed history to know what had happened where I was. I needed maths to count the days I was away. I needed reading, to be able to read books and letters, and writing, in order to be able to reply to the letters, and keep a journal.

'You didn't need Irish,' I said.

'I needed Irish for the times I didn't want anyone to know what I was saying.'

I reflected on all that, for a minute.

'What are you doing for your week?' he asked.

'I'm supposed to be confined to the house,' I said, 'doing schoolwork.'

'Then you'd better get back there and do it,' he said.

I leaned over and stroked the fox, whom I'd been completely ignoring this visit, and when I took my leave of them to run home, I noticed there was a smile hiding in the man's beard. I was sure it was a smile this time.

holding the fox

I felt guilty that night about neglecting the fox. The poor little creature had little enough pleasure in his life. Oh, the man was fond enough of him, that was clear, but he didn't exactly fuss over him like most people fussed over their dogs. A little extra attention would be good for him. I resolved to make him the main focus of my visit next time.

I'd surprised myself, though – and my mum – by the amount of work I'd done. What the man had said about needing school even to be a sailor had impressed me. I'd never thought of school in that way. I'd spent most time on geography, as knowing the man had been to all those places had brought the subject alive for me, but I did a little bit in every subject – a day is a long time – even maths, which I'd always hated. At this rate, my mum said, I'd soon be top of the class. I doubted that!

I also did some drawing. I imagined the man on the prow of his ship, passing a desert island. I didn't know what flag to draw on his ship, so I left it blank. It wasn't a very big ship, but it had two backward-sloping funnels, and two lifeboats, covered in tarpaulin. Portholes were easier to draw than ordinary windows, I discovered, and I had fun with the seagulls flying overhead. After I'd drawn the seagulls, I wondered if seagulls flew as far south as desert islands, but I figured they must fly everywhere. I found it hard to draw the man without the fox, as I'd only ever seen them together, but the man had told me he hadn't known the fox when he was a sailor, and my drawing had to be true. The next drawing I'd do would be of the fox.

I slept well that night and dreamed of school. It was night-time in the dream, and the school was empty. The only light was the moonlight coming though the window, and in this pale glow I saw the fox walk through my classroom and curl up on the floor at the foot of my desk.

The dream was so vivid that I woke up and reached down to stroke the fox. It was a strange dream that kept me thinking for a while, but I was soon asleep again.

My dad woke me, for a change, the next morning. He hadn't come in the previous night before I'd gone to sleep, and he'd heard from my mum that I'd worked well.

'I'm very pleased with you,' he said. 'Keep it up.'

As he was leaving he noticed my new drawing lying on the chair next to my bed.

'Your imagination's been working overtime,' he said.

I grinned and said nothing.

I had breakfast with my mum, who was starting work a little later that day. I asked her to boil me an egg to have after my cereal.

'Schoolwork obviously makes you hungry!' she said.

She was happy to do it for me, as she always worried that I didn't eat enough. She made me two pieces of toast, as well, without my asking for them. She herself had only a banana and a yoghurt. She was always watching her weight.

Eventually she went, though, and I wasn't long out the door after her. She wasn't the type to hide and try to catch me out. I took a small present with me for the fox – a chicken leg, leftover from last night's dinner, which I wrapped in some aluminium foil. It was only a nibble, really, but I wanted to be nice to the fox today.

When I got there the man pretended to be cross with me. I ignored him, unwrapped the chicken leg and held it in front of the fox's nose. It occurred to me, belatedly, that I was now giving the man a real reason to be cross with me – I hadn't thought to bring him anything!

The fox was very interested in my present. His little nose began twitching and his eyes darted from me to the chicken leg. He made a lunge for it and grabbed it with his teeth, where-upon the man lifted him down from his shoulders to allow him to clean the bone in privacy. After he'd done that he began crunching the bone, but the man took it from him, got to his feet, walked to the nearest bin and dropped it in.

'Chicken bones are dangerous,' he said. 'They splinter and could do serious damage.'

He didn't seem to be cross with me, though, for bringing the chicken leg to the fox. In fact, he seemed pleased.

As he was awkwardly sitting down in the doorway again, using the black stick as a lever, I decided to ask him a favour.

'Could I hold the fox for a minute or two?'

'Be my guest,' he said, motioning me to sit on the ground, then lifting the fox and handing him to me. He observed me very carefully as I took the fox in my arms. The fox was a little nervous, to begin with, but the man reached over and stroked him between the ears, urging me to do likewise. I did, and the fox relaxed. The man took his hand away and left us alone.

Now, I'd held a cat before, but this was different. There was none of that purring, for a start, and certainly none of that scratching with claws. The fox was slightly heavier, but not too heavy. Even through my jumper, his tail felt smooth on my arm. With my nose so close to him, though, I did notice he smelt a bit funny. I must have shown this on my face because the man laughed.

'So you've noticed Russ's foxy smell, have you? Don't worry, you'll get used to it.'

I handed him back to the man, and thanked him, then said I thought it was time I went home. The man nodded, and said he'd see me.

As I came into our street, I looked up and down but no one was paying me any attention. Just to be sure, I pretended to turn a key in the lock, before pushing the door in front of me. I clicked the snib off and ran straight upstairs to begin the drawing of me holding the fox.

scrabble

I'd barely got the drawing finished when I heard the front door open and my mum call up the stairs. What was she doing home so early? I heard her begin to come up, so I shut the drawing in a drawer and covered it with socks. I'd told her about the fox, and as soon as she saw the drawing she'd know I'd gone outside today to see it. That drawing would make her believe the fox existed but it would also get me in trouble.

I grabbed my geography book and opened it on India just as she turned the handle of the door.

'Hello Gerard,' she said. 'Are you hungry? I've got some buns. Oh, I see you're doing geography again. You must be going to travel the world.'

'I'd like to, I said. We never go anywhere.'

'Oh, maybe we will, maybe we will. What about that bun, then? I'm going down to make a cup of tea.'

It was only when she was halfway down the stairs that I remembered to ask her what she was doing home so early. She mumbled something about shift work and shut the kitchen door behind her. Why she was suddenly doing shift work was not explained to me. It was as well, I thought, that I hadn't been caught outside when she got home.

I got another surprise later that day. My dad was staying in that evening, and after dinner (chilli con carne, one of my favourites) he suggested the three of us play Scrabble. I looked at my mum and my mum looked at me. This was a turn up for the books! Of course, we agreed – even though I knew there was no chance of my winning, and I never liked losing at anything.

My mum was ahead for most of the game, and I hoped she would win, but my Dad got rid of all his seven letters in a corner triple word and scored so high he couldn't be caught. You should have heard the whoops of him. I was last all the way, but I did have one pleasing moment – I managed to put an F in front of the Ox my dad had put down. Unfortunately, he'd already got the triple score for the X, but still.

I decided there and then that before I was twelve years old I'd beat my dad at Scrabble. I'd have to practise. Maybe my mum would play with me when my dad was out. (I'd ask her not to tell my dad about these practice sessions – I wanted him to get a surprise when I beat him.) Maybe I could bring the board out and play with the man with the fox. I'd say, with all his travelling, he'd be good at Scrabble. I could already imagine the stares we'd get, sitting on the pavement, with the Scrabble board between us.

moody

I quizzed my mum the next morning about what shifts she was on all week, but when I saw her noticing my unusual interest in the matter I changed the subject to what we were having for dinner that evening. I didn't want her getting suspicious and telling me lies, so she could check up on whether I stayed in the house or not. So far I didn't think either she or my dad had any suspicions. I wanted to keep it that way.

As I approached the man, I saw straight away he was moody. The fox seemed edgy too, perhaps as a consequence. I felt immediately unwelcome.

'Are you not happy today?' I asked the man.

'No,' was the blunt reply.

'What's wrong? Are you not feeling well?'

'What's it to you?' said the man.

I was a bit shocked and disappointed at this, but I said nothing in response. I looked down at the beret – there was very little money in it, but I didn't think this had anything to do with the man's mood.

'Why don't you go home and do your schoolwork?' he said, and lifted the fox to the ground, before pointing to me and saying to the fox:

'Go, get him, Russ. Send him running home.'

But the fox just stood there, looking at the man. He gave me one brief glance but it was the man he preferred to look at.

Then the man gave a deep sad laugh, and said:

'Oh, Gerard Lavelle, it's not your fault I hate the world today. Come and sit with the fox and me.'

I sat down with them. I was glad and relieved to be invited to do so, but I knew there would be little conversation that day, and I wouldn't stay long. I'd wanted to ask the man if he'd ever played Scrabble, and where he'd suggest I go the first time I went abroad. I'd leave that till another time.

It was so awkward sitting there that I was about to get up and leave when the man surprised me with an invitation I'd never expected.

'Would you like to take the fox for a walk?'

'What? I said.

'Yes, a short walk, to the end of the street and back.'

'You bet!' I said.

I got to my feet, and the man motioned the fox to go with me. The fox stood motionless, looking at the man for a minute, but eventually came to me. I hesitated but the man urged me on.

'Go on, Gerard Lavelle. You don't need a lead. The fox will stay close to your feet.'

So we set off, me and the fox. He was slightly in front of me, and the long shadow of his tail fell across me. I felt very proud walking with such a beautiful animal, and I ignored all the stares we were attracting. When we got to the end of the street I stopped and the fox stopped too, then we retraced our steps until we were back at the man. It was over too soon.

His eyes had been closed as we approached but he opened them again, gave a tired smile and stroked the fox's head.

'Thank you very much,' I said. 'I'll be off now, I think. I'll come back when you're feeling better.'

I turned back once halfway down the street, after I'd said goodbye to them, and the man raised his arm and gave a small slow wave. I didn't like seeing him sad like that. It must be hard, I thought, coming to sit in a doorway day after day.

gone

When I got to the doorway the following morning, it was empty. No man, no fox. I hung around for a while, repeatedly glancing down the street, but there was no sign of them. I was shocked to see that one of the windows of the shop whose doorway they sat in was smashed. Had the man's mood made him do that? He'd never struck me as a violent person. Or had someone else thrown something at the man and missed? Reluctantly I went home, tried to read my Irish language storybook but couldn't concentrate.

Three times during the morning, and once during the afternoon I went back there, to no avail. They weren't going to show today. Remembering how sad the man had been the day before, I was very worried. Was he too depressed to come out? What would he and the fox do for food?

Or was he sick? I'd heard my mum say there was a bad flu going round. I remembered that just before I'd come down with flu the year before I'd been gloomy and quiet for a day or two. But then I'd had my mum there to look after me – to buy me lucozade, give me hot lemon drinks and sweets to suck for my sore throat, and come up to my bedroom every now and then to keep me company. The man had no one except the fox.

I thought again about the way the man had been. That was not gloominess before a flu. It was more serious than that. And didn't depressed people sometimes kill themselves – and kill those they loved, as well?

I should go to see him. But I didn't know where he lived, or where to begin looking. Talk about looking for a needle in a haystack – with a city this size, it was more like looking for the snapped-off point of a needle in the haystack. Besides, I was still under house arrest. It was one thing slipping out briefly to go to the next street, it was another thing altogether to go off searching through streets I didn't know.

And how would I find the pair of them anyway? Say, they lived in a house or a hostel somewhere – I could be right outside and I wouldn't know they were in there. Without x-ray eyes it was useless.

My thoughts were running away with themselves. I forced myself to remember that the man and the fox hadn't showed up one other day, yet they were back the day after. It would be the same this time. I'd go there tomorrow morning and there they'd be, and I'd feel stupid for the way I'd felt today.

I took out all the drawings I'd done of the man or of the fox. I propped them up all round my dressing table, starting with the man looking happy and young on his ship, and finishing with the most recent one – of me walking with the fox. It didn't really look like me, I thought, but l was getting better at drawing the fox. I stared at the fox through half-closed eyes, as if in a trance, willing it to tell me where it was. It wouldn't.

I lay on the bed, then, looking at the ceiling. I wished it was bedtime, and I was about to fall asleep. I wished it was morning, and my Mum was waking me. I even almost wished I was at school.

foxless, manless

The rest of that week, including the week-end, stayed foxless and manless. It was the slowest week I'd ever lived through. Again and again I went round to the shop doorway but it stayed empty, and each time I approached it, I expected less and less to find them sitting there. Soon I began to wonder if they'd ever been there – had I dreamed the whole thing up? My dad was always saying I had too much imagination for my own good. Maybe my Mum was right when she'd said you don't find foxes in cities.

But no, I remembered very clearly the man's face and beard. I remembered the fox's little eyes and his huge brush of a tail. I remembered holding him, and the looks on people's faces when I'd taken him for a walk. I couldn't imagine that well.

So I brooded in my room most of the time. I doodled in my notebook but couldn't do any real drawings. I did hardly any more school-work. My mum was worried about me but I didn't care. She asked me what the matter was but I didn't tell her. At mealtimes I picked at my food – even when Mum made spaghetti with prawns specially for me on Friday evening. On Saturday afternoon my dad got cross with me and made me come down and sit with them in the living room. He couldn't make me talk, though.

It was a relief to set off for school on Monday morning. I was a bit nervous after the week off, and what had happened last time, so I got there very early. My dad had warned me that if I got into any more trouble I'd be grounded for the rest of the year. It was still only October!

I stayed by myself in the corner of the play-ground while the other children filed in. The boy who'd been in the fight with me arrived, along with one of his friends, but he didn't even look at me. His dad must have warned him, too.

At assembly the Headteacher embarrassed me by bringing up the fight again, and telling us all that the next fight that came to his attention would result in the pugilists being expelled from the school. I didn't know the word 'pugilists' but I could guess what it meant. The Head stared right at me, not at the other boy, as he said this, and I could feel the eyes of all the other children on me. The heat of my face told me I was blushing. The Head then read out a poem about bullying, and said that there would be no bullying in this school.

As I settled into my seat in the classroom I thought how unfair the whole thing was. I wasn't a bully. That's not what the fight had been about. I'd only been defending myself – the other boy had started it. I was still feeling hard done by when the class teacher came and stood in front of me.

'We're glad to see you back, Gerard, after your week's holiday. Did you go somewhere nice?'

She gave a little laugh, that some of the children joined in with. Then, more seriously,

'What's this grumpy face all about? Cheer up – it can't be that bad being back among us.'

And I did cheer up when I saw that geography was the first subject we were doing. The teacher drew a map on the board. Before she'd finished I could see it was South America. She divided it into the various countries, pointed at one and asked what it was. I stuck my hand up immediately.

'Argentina, Miss.'

'Good, Gerard. And what is the capital of Argentina?'

'Buenos Aires, Miss.'

'Excellent, Gerard. You clearly haven't been wasting your week away.'

I had the man to thank for that, I said to myself.

the plan

Nobody bothered me that day at school and I bothered no one either. I kept to myself, and the other kids seemed happy to let me. That suited me. The combination of the public warning from the Headteacher, and the fact that I'd won the two fights I'd been in, seemed to make everyone afraid to come near me. Good.

I spent much of the day thinking about what I could do to track down the man and the fox. I had to find them, I knew that. But how? I decided to draw up a plan.

It had to be a plan in various stages. First, there was a possibility the man and the fox would be back in the doorway when I got to it on my way home. I didn't think they would be, but it was always possible. I wouldn't just go straight there, though. I'd go home via a big detour, through streets I'd never visited before. They had to be somewhere – and considering the man's limp, somewhere not too far away, I figured. The man had even told me they lived not too far away.

My zigzag search was fruitless, and they were not in their doorway, either. My mum was waiting for me at home.

'You're late,' she said. 'What kept you? Not more trouble at school, I hope?'

'No, Mum. I took a different route home, that's all, and got a bit lost.'

'Silly boy,' she said. 'What's wrong with the route I discovered? It's the shortest.'

'Yes, Mum.'

I went upstairs to think out the next stages of the plan. I would keep coming home from school by different routes, but I had to think of something else. What could that something be?

Who did the man know, or more to the point, who knew him? Everybody was known by someone. And the man did stand out somewhat, going everywhere with a fox. Someone must have noticed the two of them leaving and coming back to wherever they lived.

I thought of writing out a sign saying *Has anyone seen a man with a fox?* and walking with it through the streets, but I didn't quite feel up to that, yet. I'd keep it back as a later possibility – a further stage of the plan that we might not have need of. There had to be an easier way.

I could put an ad in the newspaper but I knew ads cost money, and all I had was my pocket money. For a minute I thought it was time to bring my mother in on all this, but no, all she'd do is forbid me to have any furthur contact with the man and the fox.

I had to continue alone.

Then, suddenly, I had an idea. The man must know other people who were on the streets, and they must know him. My mum had told me that soup kitchens came round to give free soup and bread to all the homeless. Maybe some people on the streets around here shared a hostel, or a shelter with the man and the fox. Maybe there was a bush telegraph among people like that that told them when one of their kind was in trouble.

I knew immediately that this was the way to go about it. I should have thought of it earlier. I would approach as many people as possible on my way home from school the next day. Surely one of them would know. I hoped it was not too late.

mr hannigan

My first interview the next afternoon was with a man who introduced himself immediately, quite formally, as Mr Hannigan, and seemed very happy to talk to me. He was an oldish man with stubble, and he wore a very frayed-looking tweed overcoat, but underneath this I saw he was wearing a tie. He was sitting on a pile of cardboard boxes in the opening of an alleyway, and when I approached him he put down the book he was reading, and took his wire-rimmed glasses off.

'And what do they call you, young man?' he asked.

I said my name, and he motioned me to sit down beside him, but I didn't know him, so I stayed standing up. Besides, I'd already detected a faint smell of pee, although this could have come from the alleyway.

'Do you read much, Gerard?' Mr Hannigan continued.

I shook my head.

'What? I read all the time,' he said, very firmly.

He picked up the book and waved it in front of me.

'I've always read, even when I was your age. Libraries are wonderful establishments. You can travel the whole world, and live many different lives, when you read books.'

I promised to join the local library and begin reading more, just to get him off the subject. He sounded for all the world like a teacher – maybe he had been a teacher, or a librarian. I'd had enough of teachers for the moment, and anyway I had something to ask him.

'Do you know a man with a fox? He's a man who spends time on the streets, like you – a man with long hair and a beard. Anyway, he's disappeared. I thought you might know him.'

Mr Hannigan shook his head. 'A man with a fox? Remarkable! I would certainly remember such a sight. But alas, dear Gerard, I have not seen him. I'm only lately arrived in this fine city.'

'I'll say goodbye, then.' I said, wanting to get on.

'Good day to you, Gerard. And remember the books.'

I looked round once as I walked away and there he was, back at his reading. It must be a good book to be able to be read like that, out on the street.

the end of the world man

In the very next street I saw a man coming towards me, wearing a placard saying *The End of the World is Upon Us*. This was written in big red letters. If he'd meant it to scare passers-by it didn't seem to be working. People were ignoring it, or barely suppressing smiles.

Every now and again he'd emphasise his message by calling out in a high-pitched voice, 'Repent, you sinners, or you'll all go to HELL!'

This didn't have the intended effect, either. After one such outburst, a coin or something came flying through the air and clattered off the placard on to the street. The result of this was a loud repetition of 'You'll all go to Hell!', then silence. He didn't look round to see who'd thrown the coin, or bend down to pick it up.

By the time he came to me, or I came to him,

he seemed quite calm. His eyes even caught mine, although they held no expression. His face was small and pinched, like a bird's.

I decided to ask him my question.

'Excuse me, sir, have you seen a man with a fox?'

He reacted with a start, as if he wasn't used to being spoken to.

'A fox? The Devil's creature! And any man who'd have one must be a devil himself. He belongs in hell.'

I immediately regretted ever talking to him. I hurried away and didn't speak to anyone else until I got home.

the composition

The following morning in school, our teacher asked us to write a composition. She wanted us to imagine being someone else, and try to write that person's story. It could be someone real or someone made up, but she wanted us to make that person a bit different.

So I wrote about being a sailor who went all over the world, and who decided to settle for a while in Africa. I remembered from my atlas the name Cape Town, so that was where I had the sailor live. I'd seen a programme about lions on the TV not long ago, and I had the sailor go on safari so he could take pictures of lions. I thought about letting him have a pet lion cub, but I didn't know if people were allowed to have lion cubs as pets, even in Africa. And what would happen when the lion cub grew?

Instead, I made his lion photographs get famous, and had the sailor start making films of the lions, films that began appearing on televisions all over the world. This caused a problem in my composition, as I'd started off imagining I was the man with the fox, before he'd met the fox, but now I was a different man, one who was too famous and successful in Africa to come back to Ireland and live rough on the streets of a city, with a fox. The composition story had gone in its own direction. As Mr Hannigan had said, it had created a different life.

I was finished before the end of the lesson, so I drew pictures to accompany my story. I loved drawing the male lions with their big hairy manes, but my lion cubs were a bit too much like cats. When the bell went, I handed the teacher my composition and went out to the playground. The sky was grey again, and looked like rain. I wished I was under the blue sky of Africa.

smiler

I was beginning to feel guilty about not making any headway in finding the man with the fox, so I decided to try harder. The man might be in trouble, and one day might make a difference in whether he could be helped or not. I would talk to at least three people on the streets on my way home, and I wouldn't allow myself to be put off again.

Right outside the school gates I came across a happy-looking, red-faced man sitting propped up in a doorway, drinking wine from a bottle. I walked past him, at first, because I didn't want the other kids or any of the teachers see me talking to him. They wouldn't understand why I'd want to.

So I went off up a quiet street that came to a dead end, then doubled back slowly and waited

70

till I was sure everybody had left the school. Then I walked over to the man.

'Hello,' I said, 'how are you doing?'

'Ah, a schoolboy,' said the man. 'I'm doing very well, ducky. Very well, indeed.'

He beamed a big smile at me, and took another swig of wine.

'Want some?' he asked, pretending to offer me the bottle. 'No, of course not, you're too young. Besides, I wouldn't want to waste any.' He smiled again, and accompanied this with a laugh.

'Know what they call me?' he said. 'Smiler. That's me, Smiler. I'm always happy, that's why.'

This was encouraging. 'Well, Smiler,' I said hopefully. 'Maybe you can help me. I'm looking for a man with a fox.'

'A man with a fox, ducky? Yes, I've seen the pair of them about. Grumpy-looking fellow with long hair and a beard. Doesn't speak much. He used to be there when the soup came. Haven't seen him in a while, though.'

'And you don't know where they live?' I asked.

'Live, ducky? They could live anywhere in this big city.'

And Smiler threw his head back and laughed again, and afterwards fixed his smile on me, before stopping it with the mouth of the wine bottle. This time he kept it there, as if he meant to drain the bottle dry.

annie may

Although I'd noticed that most of the people on the streets were men, every now and again I'd come across a woman. There was one I'd seen sitting by the fountain in the park, selling postcards she'd put a few daubs of paint on. I'd looked at a couple of these one day but hadn't thought much of them.

Anyway, I thought she was worth checking out, so I made a bee-line for the park.

The woman was there again, so I went up to her. She turned her face to me but decided I wasn't worth bothering with, and instead went back to scrutinising the faces of passers by.

I picked up a postcard of a tightrope walker – a young woman, on to whose head had been painted a red hat. I put it back, and picked up another – a harbour scene that now included a

73

large yellow fish. There seemed to be about fifty postcards there in all, each with one little addition in a different coloured paint. I didn't see the point, myself, but I supposed it was better than expecting money for nothing.

While I was there, a man dropped a fifty pence coin into a cup without taking a postcard. The woman seemed to recognise him and nodded. She didn't seem to mind that he hadn't wanted a postcard.

I decided to pretend to be considering buying a postcard. I picked out one of a man lying in a hammock, with purple sunglasses painted on to his face.

'How much is this?' I asked.

The woman pointed to a handpainted sign that was lying on the ground at the top of the postcards. It said *'Annie May's Postcards – £1 each.'* One pound that was a lot! I put my hand in my pocket but all I had was forty-five pence. I looked at it, looked at the woman, shrugged, and went to put the postcard back:

'I'm sorry, I haven't got enough money,' I said politely.

'How much have you got?' she asked.

'Forty-five pence,' I replied.

'That'll do,' she said. 'I'll take it.'

As I was handing her the money I decided I'd earned my question this time.

'I don't suppose you've seen a man with a fox?'

Annie May looked surprised. 'No, but they'd make a great postcard.'

'You haven't seen them?' I persisted.

She shook her head. 'They sure as hell haven't come by here. I'd remember.'

I reckoned she would, so I took my postcard and left her. Where did she get all those postcards, I wondered. They must cost money to buy. I felt guilty that I hadn't had the right money, but at the same time forty-five pence was quite a lot of money for me. There were other, better things I could have bought with it. I looked at the postcard again and asked myself what I could do with it. I didn't even like it much. I thought of dropping it in a bin but decided that would be wrong. Instead, I thought I might try and use it for drawing practice.

asleep on the bench

As I was heading out of the park, I saw a young man I recognised lying asleep on a bench. He was one of the youngest homeless I'd seen – he couldn't have been more than eighteen, if he was that. The first time I'd seen him, I'd wondered what had happened at home to make him go on the streets so young. Had he had a huge row with his mum or dad? Did they know where he was? I'd wanted to speak to him but when he'd seen me staring at him he'd scowled and told me to go away.

I'd last come across him a day or two before, but he looked very different now. His left wrist was in plaster, and his nose was clearly broken. Someone must have beaten him up. I'd heard him once shouting at some boys who were taunting him, but he hadn't struck me as aggressive. Just sad. I'd be sad if I had to go on the streets at that age. Now he was sore as well as sad.

I stood there a while, waiting for him to wake up, but then I decided maybe this wasn't a good idea. The last thing he'd want to wake up to was a question from me about whether he'd seen a man with a fox. He probably wouldn't have noticed them anyway.

So I left him in peace, hoping his wrist would heal soon. Perhaps the beating would make him decide to go home again. Somehow, seeing how many people were on the streets, I wasn't that hopeful.

the one-legged englishman

The third and final person I spoke to that day was a one-legged Englishman who occupied the space at the foot of the statue of De Valera in the nearest main square to where we lived. It was a plum spot to be stationed in, I thought, and the amount of coins and notes in the old wooden clog he kept there for his takings seemed to prove this. It was certainly far more than I'd ever seen in the beret of the man with the fox.

I figured the wooden leg was a help with getting money. People would be feeling sorry for the man because he'd lost a leg, and as a consequence would be generous. Or at least that's what I thought. He was dressed pretty niftily, too, with a polka dotted scarf round his neck and a white carnation in the button hole of his smart black jacket. He was making it as hard as possible not to give him money. I was only sorry I had none left to give him.

'I wonder if you could help me,' I said. 'I'm looking for two friends of mine, a man and a fox.'

'Oh, yes, I've seen them,' he said. 'They make a colourful duo. But as to where they are? Alas, my young friend, I cannot help you.'

I hadn't heard many English people speak, apart from those on television, and I liked the way this man spoke. It was like cake.

'When did you last see them?' I asked.

'They used to pass by here every morning and evening,' he said. 'The man would nod to me and I would nod back. We are brothers in misfortune, are we not? He would not waste time in small talk. I last saw them over a week ago. I have been wondering where they are.'

'What direction did they come from,' I asked. This was the nearest I'd got to finding out where they might be.

The man pointed to the right hand corner of the square.

'That's the direction,' he said. 'They must live somewhere up there.'

'What's there? I asked.'

'Oh, nothing very salubrious,' the Englishman said, with a chuckle. 'A cemetery, and a dump. I hope they don't live in either of those.'

I thanked him most sincerely for this very important information, then apologised to him for having no money left to put in his clog.

'Think nothing of it, dear boy. As you can see, I'm not doing too badly today. You will let me know, won't you, if you track them down?'

I promised him I would, then skipped away. This was an exciting lead, and I wanted to head off immediately in the direction the man had indicated, but I was already very late and my mother would be worried and possibly angry. I'd done enough for one day. Tomorrow would be worth waiting for.

a writer

I wanted to bunk off school the following morning, but after the recent trouble there, and the way my parents – and the Headteacher – had reacted, I didn't want to risk further punishment. It was so tantalising, though, to know that all I had to do was turn away at the school gates and the whole day was there to spend in searching. It was unusually fine weather, too.

Grumpily, I sat down at my table and prepared myself for a long frustrating day. As soon as the final bell went I would be out the door and heading back to the square where I'd spoken to the one-legged Englishman. I needed to go there first to take my bearings.

I wasn't prepared for what was to happen in the classroom, though. The teacher stood there with a pile of our English exercise books. The compositions. In my concern to find the man and the fox I'd forgotten about the one I'd written. She proceeded to hand the exercise books out, one by one, occasionally offering comments such as 'nice characterisation' or 'a very funny story', though generally it was 'good' or 'well done'. A couple of people, she said, had only half-done the job and needed to go back and finish it. I had to wait until all the others had been given back, and instead of saying anything about mine, she asked me to read it to the class.

It was the last thing I wanted to do but she gave me no option. She even made me come up to the front of the class and stand beside her and read it from there. So, I read it out, and to my surprise the others in the class seemed to listen, and even seemed to like it. Some of them actually said so afterwards. The teacher was very complimentary.

'That was excellent, Gerard. You're a born writer.'

I blushed and went back to my seat, but I was pleased she liked it so much – especially as there was a bit of the man I was looking for in the character I'd written about. Maybe this would bring good luck to the search.

where the crutch pointed

At the final bell I wasted no time in heading for the square, and as I caught sight of the Englishman he picked up his crutch and pointed it in the direction he wanted me to go in. He also lifted the black hat he was wearing today and put it back on his head again. I gave him a cheery wave.

I hurried into a wide, quiet street I'd never been in before. There were no shops in it, nothing but terraced houses on both sides, and black ornate lampposts. Apart from myself, there were hardly any other people walking there, and even fewer cars going up and down. A taxi went by with its light on, but the driver didn't act as if he expected anyone on either pavement to signal him to stop.

It was a relief to see something as normal as a

dog coming towards me, nose to the ground – a black terrier with a green collar on. He obviously lived nearby, since he was out on his own like this. I could have used a dog to help me in the search, I reflected. One sniff of anything that had come in contact with the man, or even more so, the fox, and the dog would have led me to them immediately. My jumper would probably be enough, even though it was over a week since I'd held the fox.

I continued down the street. It was much longer than any of the streets round where I lived. Was this really the right place to come? I would have to ask the next person I met where the cemetery was – that seemed the place to make for first.

A man was coming towards me and I was about to call out to him when I noticed he was blind. How would he be able to direct me? The tapping of his white stick got louder as he approached, and I noticed he muttered something interrmittently to himself. He didn't seem happy.

I decided to let him go past me without

speaking to him, but he stopped, quite close to me stuck his head out to listen, and proceeded to cross the road. Instinctively I went to take his arm to lead him across, as my mum had always told me I should do with blind people. He brushed my hand away, however, saying; 'I can cross the road by myself, thank you!'

Embarrassed, I scuttled off, as fast as I could. That was the last time I'd ever offer to help a blind person. Ahead, I noticed some tall railings, then I saw that finally I'd come to the cemetery. I kept going till I came to the gate.

city of the dead

It was the most enormous cemetery I had ever seen – much bigger than the whole town I had moved from. It was like a city of the dead. I walked between rows of graves, wondering at the number of people who'd died. Some of the gravestones showed details of children my age or younger. I would hate to be lying here.

Most of the dates on the stones were old, but every now and again there was a more recent date, though nothing in the 21st century, I was glad to see. Further in, the graves became tombs, and some of these had very elaborate carvings, or even statues – the one I liked best was of a dog who had been so inconsolable at his master's death that he'd lain on the grave till he too died.

I bet the fox would do the same if the man

died. Immediately, I regretted thinking this, and thought I'd better get out of this place. But it was just possible the man and fox lived here – it was quiet enough, no one would bother them. Maybe there was a large, empty tomb or family vault in some overgrown corner. It wouldn't be the first time someone alive had chosen such a place as a home, I figured.

After peering at some of the bigger tombs and vaults, and finding none of them broken in, I began to feel I was on the wrong track. One tomb had a huge mound of fresh wreaths outside it, that was the only sign of a recent inhabitant I saw. And the cemetery was too big to get round – I didn't want to be caught in here after dark. If I drew a blank elsewhere I'd come back and force myself to do a meticulous search, but this was enough for now.

I walked briskly to the gate and clanged it after me, as if I didn't want anyone in there following me out.

the street of crashed cars

Rather than going back the way I'd come, I carried on along the railings until the graves were replaced by houses again. Back in the territory of the living, I thought, though there wasn't exactly much sign of life yet. It was as if either side of the cemetery was a preparation for what was to be found there.

I came to a T-junction where the road went left and right. I chose the right – the farthest away from the cemetery – and followed it until a smaller road branched off it left. I noticed that the first cars parked there were badly squashed and crumpled. They couldn't still be driveable. I crossed and went into this smaller road. There were cars parked on both sides all the way up it, and they all seemed to have been involved in crashes. It was a street of crashed cars! But why? How had they got here?

I looked at the houses on either side of the street but they seemed normal enough. Where did the people who lived there park their cars? It would have been more appropriate if these crashed cars had been parked outside the cemetery. What was the reason for them being here?

I carried on up the street past more and more crashed cars. Did so many people get involved in crashes? Why couldn't they learn to drive better? I would become a very good driver when I grew up. The road curved to the right and I saw in front of me a gigantic dump, at the entrance of which a large bonfire was blazing. I kept going. The last vehicle was a crashed van – but only the cab of the van had been squashed, the long back was intact. And sitting there in the open doorway, warming themselves by the fire, were the man and the fox.

hibernation time

The relief I felt at finding them at last must have been all over my face but the man didn't seem to notice. I told myself he was pleased to see me, but was pretending not to be. He wouldn't look at me for a while, then slowly – and it seemed, reluctantly – turned round. The fox just stared at me from the outset.

'So, you found us?' the man said grumpily. 'Bit of a detective, aren't you? I knew you'd be looking.'

Despite his tone, I smiled at the compliment.

'I was worried,' I said. 'Thought you might be sick or something.'

'It's getting late in the year, son. Almost hibernation time.'

This surprised me. It didn't seem a believable reason for leaving the shopfront. Anyway, did foxes hibernate? Whatever the truth about foxes, people didn't. I said this to the man.

'There you go again, Gerard Lavelle, taking me literally. No, we don't go to sleep for the winter, but we don't sit there on the street, either. Far too cold for that. Better to sit here at the bonfire.'

'But nobody comes by here to give you money,' I said.

'No, they don't, but I've got a bit saved up from the other seasons. And I struggle along to the soup kitchen sometimes. Other times, social services come here with warm food. For me, that is.' Here he swept his hand over the dump. 'There are plenty of rats out there to keep the fox happy.'

Neither the fox nor he looked starved, but I wasn't convinced, either, that sitting there, half in and half out of the van, in front of the bonfire, was a great way to spend your days. And the man couldn't keep the bonfire going all night. They must get very cold sleeping in the van. I thought sitting in the shop-front, with the beret half-full with coins and notes on the ground in front of them, was a better lifestyle. At least they could leave the shopfront every evening and go home to a change of scene – a bit like going home from work. Now the scene never changed.

'Come and join us in front of the fire,' the man said, moving up a bit and making room for me.

I did this, and immediately the heat of the bonfire went all through me. The prospect of sitting here for hours suddenly seemed more attractive.

The man leaned down and took what looked like bits of a broken chair from a pile he had at the van's back wheel and threw them on the fire.

'Plenty more where that came from,' he said with a chortle. 'That's the beauty of living by a dump. And it's not just bits of wood that burn, either. We get a variety of fires here.'

He made an ostentatious show of warming his hands. While he was doing this I picked up the fox and held him again. I didn't think the man would mind, and he didn't. It was good to feel the fox's warmth on top of the warmth from the bonfire. This time I hardly noticed his smell

I decided I'd stayed long enough, and it was time I went home. The man seemed happy enough, as did the fox, and now that I knew where they were I could return as often as I liked. And I would return very soon. I told them that as I headed off down past all the crashed cars.

the collection

Next day I remembered to ask the man about the crashed cars. He seemed very amused by the question, as if there was nothing more natural than a street of crashed cars.

'They're waiting their turn to be crushed,' he said with a laugh. 'It'll come to them all in time, but they have to wait.'

'Where do they get crushed?' I asked.

'Over there,' he said, 'at the far end of the dump. One by one they're lifted there, to the crusher, and they come out the size of a shoe-box. But a very, very heavy shoe-box. You wouldn't want it to fall on you.'

He laughed again at this, and continued filling me in on what went on.

'As soon as one's taken away, another one takes its place. There's no shortage of crashed cars. I check them all out when they first arrive. They contribute to my collection.'

He paused there and waited for my inevitable question.

'What collection?'

'Ah yes, my collection. It should be in a museum, young Lavelle. You, as an artist, will appreciate what I'm going to show you.

He climbed inside the van and began bringing out a series of items gleaned from cars. There was a number plate C1234. There was a blue triangular steering wheel and a round mirror. There were four hubcaps inlaid with green glass mosaics. There was a brown leather seat the man said he sat out in during the summer. There was a car radio he switched on and Irish music spilled out. There was a gear-lever, the knob of which was carved to look like a woman in a swimsuit.

I was impressed, and I told him so. The fox looked impressed, too, the way he followed intently each thing that was being produced.

'I have other stuff, too, from the dump,' he said, and proceeded to bring out some of these items. The first was a plastic leg, and this was followed by a child's pram. What he wanted with either of those was a mystery to me. The next thing was a fishing rod he said he caught birds with, to eat. I didn't believe him. Then a buoy from the sea, a black bat-box and an ancient wooden-handled golf-club. Seeing I wasn't as impressed with these as with the car stuff, he left it at that. There couldn't have been room for much more in the van anyway, I thought.

He'd given me an idea, though. A collection of my own – exactly what I'd collect I didn't know yet. It wasn't as good as drawing, but the man was right – it was a kind of art, too. I thanked him and took my leave of the two of them.

kinds of art

I was wandering round the house, scrutinising anything I saw for its collectibility. There was nothing that struck me as interesting enough. The nearest were the old family photos that my mum, in particular, had in frames all over the house. Photos were interesting – or at least, could be interesting. I thought of Annie May's postcards. As far as I was concerned, though, the best things to collect were paintings, and my parents didn't have a single one on our walls! I'd asked them about this once and my dad had said original paintings were very expensive, and if he couldn't have originals he wouldn't lower himself by putting up cheap reproductions. I hoped I would make enough money when I was older to buy loads and loads of paintings. I wanted my house to be like a gallery.

I gave up and went looking for someone to talk to. Normally I enjoyed my own company but I was getting used to my brief conversations with the man who had the fox. It was him I wanted to talk to now, naturally, but I couldn't go to him – my mother was already giving me a hard time for coming home from school late every day, so one or other of my parents would have to do instead.

I tried my dad first. He didn't talk to me as much as Mum, but he was capable of interesting conversations about surprising things. A few weeks ago he was telling me about an ice hotel and other odd goings-on in the Arctic, and got me imagining what it would be like to live where there was no daylight in winter. When I saw him sitting at the coffee table, with his glasses on and his calculator in his hand, and pages with scribbled figures on them in front of him, I knew I was out of luck today.

My mum was in the kitchen cooking the dinner. Earlier, she'd baked a cake for Christmas, even though it was still over a month away. The smell had followed me through the house as I'd looked for ideas on what to collect. I quite liked Christmas cake but I preferred the smell when it was cooking. I'd still eat some, though.

'Hello, Gerard, are you at a loss for something to do?'

'Yes, Mum.'

'You're bored, aren't you? What you need is a friend.'

I wanted to tell her I had a friend – two, if you counted the fox – but I didn't think the time was right, yet.

'Tell me what happened at school today,' Mum said.

'Nothing much. We did some boring sums, and an old man, an ex-teacher in the school, our teacher told us, came in to talk to us in Irish. I couldn't understand half of it. And we heard about the thousands who died emigrating to America during the Famine.'

'No geography, though. You must be disappointed. Or writing, either. Have you written anything more since that composition your teacher liked so much?'

I shook my head.

'Seems a pity, if you can do it so well. What about the drawing, then? Are there any more masterpieces being created up in that room of yours?'

Again, I shook my head.

'Something's obviously up with you when you're not drawing. I've never known you not to draw, Gerard. Is some aspect of school bothering you again? You're not getting into more trouble fighting with other boys, are you?'

'No, Mum, I'm not.'

'I'm glad to hear it.'

She was slicing chicken breasts very thinly and putting the slices on to a plate. Alongside were other plates with slices of red pepper, green chillis, spring onions, and finely chopped garlic and ginger on them. I liked watching my mum cook, and seeing how the tastes were made. Cooking was a kind of art, too, I thought. I knew I'd be able to cook when I grew up.

the man who collects skulls

I didn't go to see the man and the fox again till the weekend. It was raining all the time, and one day my mum came and collected me from school, like she used to do, and anyway, I was very busy at home, writing and drawing. Yes, I had a new story – one that had been prompted by a very vivid dream I'd had the night after the man had shown me his collection.

I'd dreamed about a large collection of skulls, and when I woke up because of the dream I couldn't get back to sleep again. It wasn't that I was frightened – these skulls weren't human, they were animal and bird – just that the dream hadn't told me everything and I was trying to imagine the rest. So there in bed, in the dark, the story began to grow.

I decided the collection belonged to a man

who lived alone in a big house in the country. He was a rich man who travelled a lot, all over the world, on business. I had to come up with a name for him and the only one that came into my head was John Johns. He'd go to America, say, see an eagle skull in a shop that sold those kind of things, and peel off some dollars from a roll. He wouldn't take the skull away with him – no, he'd pay to have the skull posted to him in a box. Or he'd see a dead wolf lying, half-eaten, in the woods and he'd pay someone to clean off the skull and send it to him. In the beginning he only collected small skulls but gradually they began to get bigger, so one day a long box came with a horse's skull in it, and another day a huge box, with *fragile* written all over it, containing a moose's skull, complete with antlers. And soon he didn't have to go looking for these skulls, or even to buy them – people knew he collected them and would send them to him as presents.

He had to have a special room for these skulls, of course, so he took the bed out of the big downstairs guest-room and had the walls and ceiling painted black. Then he had small spotlights fitted all over, and put the skulls on stands and tables, each with its own light trained on it. The whole thing looked beautiful, and Johns loved showing it to guests. They were always very impressed, even those who didn't want to stay in the room long. There was still room for new exhibits, but more skulls would come in all the time, and soon he'd need to convert a second room.

I asked myself what had made him start this collection, and decided he'd had three different dogs as a boy – a cocker spaniel and two red setters – and they'd all been killed by cars. He'd insisted on burying these dogs in his garden, and once after a week of extremely heavy rain, the skull of one of the red setters, Oscar, had been brought to the surface again. So he'd washed it off, and taken it up to his bedroom. Later he'd dug up and added the skulls of the two other dogs, and these three skulls were the beginning of his collection.

I wrote all this, and it took me most of the week, and came to twelve pages. Some of the pages, or bits of them, were taken up with drawings of the skulls, and of the black room. I found skulls hard to get right and had to go to the school library to find books with skull illustrations in them, so I could practise. I finished the story over the weekend, and decided not to show it to Mum or Dad until my teacher had seen it first. I'd bring it in to show her on Monday.

the woman who left

Saturday morning was dry, my mum was out shopping, my dad was having a lie-in, so even though I still had some of my story to write, I decided to go and visit the man and the fox. I went on my bike and I took small gifts for both of them, one of Dad's cans of beer (he had so many in the fridge he wouldn't miss one), and two raw sausages which I wrapped in a kitchen towel.

It was the first time I'd gone by bike to visit them in their winter home, and it made it a lot quicker to get there. The bonfire was blazing, as usual, and I thought, as I approached, that if the fox wanted the sausages cooked, we could just prong them on a stick and roast them, but I was sure the fox wouldn't care that they were raw. In fact, he would probably prefer it.

They looked as if they were expecting me – or at least, there was no surprise displayed at my arrival. I gave them the gifts immediately, unwrapping the sausages and leaving them in front of the fox, then handing the man the beer. I was not prepared for his reaction.

'Thank you, Gerard, but no thank you. I don't drink any more.'

I took the can and put it back in my pannier. The man looked at me and looked into the fire.

'My drinking cost me a good woman,' he said.

I didn't understand him. My dad drank, but so did my mum. Most of their friends drank, too.

'Did she not drink too, this woman?' I asked.

'Yes, she did. But there's drinking and there's drinking. I drank too much, and one day she left me. Packed her bags and went away.'

'Was she your wife? Did you and she have a home somewhere?'

'Yes, we did.'

'Where?'

'Somewhere far from here, Gerard.'

'Did you meet her on your travels?'

The man laughed.

'No, I met other women on my travels. I met this one later, in this country.'

He went quiet then, and stared into the fire. The fox, meanwhile, had scoffed the two sausages and was looking up at me to see if I had any more. I wished I'd brought him the whole pack.

I felt bad about bringing the man the beer. I'd made him remember his wife, and now he was sad again – and this time it was my doing. But I understood a bit more about why the man was on the streets. He had said, though, that the woman had left him. Why hadn't he stayed in the home? Had she come back and made him go away? I wanted to ask him this but I couldn't without making him more sad.

Instead, I got on my bike quietly and cycled away. I cycled slowly down past the cemetery. I was too sad myself to pedal fast. I wondered what she'd looked like, the man's wife, or where she was now. Did they have any children? He hadn't said. There was so much I didn't know about him, though I was finding out a little more all the time.

As I entered the square, I remembered the can of beer in my pannier. I couldn't bring it home, as my dad would be up now, and he would wonder what I was doing with it. I didn't want to throw it away, either. So I cycled over to the statue where the one-legged Englishman usually sat. He was there, and was glad to see me.

'Oh, hello, dear boy, did you have any luck tracking down our two friends?'

'Yes, thanks to you.'

'Glad to be of help, glad to be of help. And how are they?'

'They're fine.'

'Delighted to hear this.'

I rummaged in my pannier. 'Would you like a can of beer? As a thank you for helping me.'

'What a splendid gesture,' the Englishman said, grabbing the can and opening it, on the spot.

'Thank you,' he added, after one long swig, putting the can down on the ground until later.

'I must go,' I said. 'Bye.'

'Arrivederci, dear boy. Come by any time.'

I kicked away from the kerb and headed home. It was time i got back to the man who collected skulls.

morbid

On Monday I gave my teacher the story, and on Tuesday she called me up after class. Before she said anything I knew she didn't like it.

'What a strange imagination you have, Gerard. Where did this story come from?

'I don't know, Miss.'

Well, I did know, a bit, but I couldn't tell her about the man's collection. And she wouldn't like to hear about my dream of skulls.

'It's well-written, as I'd expect, Gerard,' she continued. 'But all this stuff about skulls? It's a bit morbid, isn't it? Someone your age shouldn't be thinking about things like that.'

She handed me back the story and went to tidy her desk. I walked out, feeling a bit disappointed by her reaction, especially as she'd liked the previous story so much. I liked this one better.

When I got home I told my mum what had happened. She asked to see the story, and sat down to read it immediately. She laughed a lot, as she was reading it.

'I think it's very good, Gerard. But your teacher has a point. It *is* morbid.'

'What's morbid, Mum?'

'Morbid? It means gloomy, thinking of death.'

'But my story isn't gloomy, Mum. And it's not about death. Those skulls aren't death – death's left them behind long ago. They're Art now.'

'Yes, Gerard,' she said laughing, giving me a hug.

I went up to my room thinking grown-ups had funny ideas sometimes, ideas that seemed wrong to me. Maybe not all grown-ups, though.

I sat down to read through my story that nobody liked except me.

calcutta and the louisiana swamps

By 3.15 on Wednesday afternoon I was back with the man and the fox. It was like going to visit relatives now, almost. I still didn't know as much about the man as I wanted to.

I peered at him when I first got there to see if he was still down but was glad to see he wasn't. I was determined not to upset him this visit, so straight away I took him back to his time as a sailor. I knew he was happy to talk about his life then.

'Tell me about your favourite city that you've ever gone to, and your favourite country place, too.'

'My favourite city? That's easy. Calcutta.'

I knew that was in India, and I liked the sound of India, so I waited for what he might say.

'Calcutta's like no other city in the whole world. There's more teeming life there than anywhere else. More people living on the streets, too. There are roadside slums and shanty towns, people washing themselves publicly at street pumps or selling all kinds of stuff along the roads – scrawny horses and goats, butcher stalls with goats' heads and other delicacies. And the crazy traffic, cars crossing lanes without warning, cutting in or coming from side roads without signals, horns blowing all the time, no traffic lights whatsoever, and kamikaze pedestrians weaving in and out through the traffic trying to get to the other side. And three kinds of rickshaws – motor, bicycle and ones pulled by men. And enormous wealth amid all the poverty – it used to be the capital of British India, and it shows. I tell you, Gerard, I never visited any city that felt so different when I first landed, or that I most wanted to return to afterwards.'

'And did you return?'

'I never did. Sadly. It never happened again.'

'What about the country place?'

'Oh, that would have to be the Louisiana swamps. Another wonderful city there, too – New Orleans, a little bit of France in America – then the swamps. Nothing but trees and water for miles and miles. And alligators! Know how the tour-guides lure them close to the boats for photographs? By chucking marshmallows into the water. The 'gators love them. The marshmallows float there and the big mouths float up and gobble them. Better a marshmallow than me, I thought. I ate alligator meat a few times – voodoo alligator, they called it. Cajun food, tasted real good. And the Cajun music, and women! A great part of the world, young Gerard. Make sure you visit it some day.'

'I will,' I said.

I was watching the fox out of the corner of my eye. He was crouching, intent on something. The man saw me watching and laughed.

'That's his dinner,' he said. 'Russ's hungry. Go for it, Russ!'

The fox was off like a rocket and I heard a squeal, then the fox came back with a rat in his mouth, which he began to devour.

'Making me hungry,' the man said, with another laugh. It wasn't making me hungry. It was making me sick! I decided it was time to go. The fact that it was perfectly natural behaviour for a fox didn't occur to me till later, when I was halfway home.

I thanked the man for his reminiscences, and headed off, wondering if he'd go to the soup kitchen or if the social services would bring him something. There wouldn't be a lot of variety in the food he ate, or taste, either, I imagined – not like Mum's cooking. I wished I could take him back with me.

the christmas play

I knew we were getting near Christmas when the Headteacher announced at assembly that we would be starting rehearsals for the Christmas play, and he asked anyone who wanted to be in it to put their hands up. I stuck my hand up automatically, though I doubted if he'd pick me. I hadn't spoken to him since our last little conversation when he'd suspended me from school for a week after the fight. And so many people put their hands up that he couldn't accommodate them all in the play. It would be very easy for him to pass me over.

He didn't pick anyone there and then but later, at lunch break, he called me aside and asked me to follow him into his room.

'I've been keeping an eye on you,' he said, 'and I've been very glad to notice your behaviour has improved considerably. I've been hearing from your class teacher about your artistic success – your drawing and writing. Do your talents extend to acting?'

'I was in the Christmas play at my last school. I played Joseph.'

'That's quite a big part, so you've had some experience. I'd like to give you the biggest part in this year's play. That's if you believe you're up to it, Gerard.'

'I think I am, Sir.'

'Good. I'd better tell you about the play. It'll be a bit different from the one at your last school. We don't do traditional plays here. We come up with a new one every year.'

'Who writes them, Sir?'

'I do, Gerard. You see, I'm a bit of a writer, too.'

This was a surprising thing to hear. I was suddenly very curious to hear what the play would be about.

'You'll be playing an alien, Gerard. A creature from another galaxy who comes down in a UFO to tell people here to stop messing up their beautiful planet.'

'An alien, Sir?' I didn't know teachers ever thought about aliens.

'Yes, an alien. We'll have great fun coming up with your costume. You might like to design it yourself.'

'And does this alien get his message across?'

'Of course, Gerard. This is a Christmas play. We have to be upbeat and positive. Run along now. We'll start rehearsals next week. And in the meantime, start thinking about what you're going to look like.'

I went out into the playground thinking two things – that school was better than it used to be, and that if an alien did come down with a message like that no one would listen to him.

cub

It was the weekend before I visited the man and the fox again, and I needed all my strength to pedal against the strong, cold wind that was in my face most of the way there. I had decided that today I was going to try and find out exactly how the man and the fox had got together. He might not tell me – just as he wouldn't tell me his name or where he was from. I would ask him the direct question anyway.

I'd asked myself that question many times and had come up with different answers, none of which seemed really possible. Had he bought the fox in a pet shop? I didn't know if foxes were ever sold in pet shops, and I'd never seen anyone else with a fox. At the same time, the man's fox was obviously not wild.

Could he have caught the fox in a trap and

gradually tamed it? Or had he some magic power over the fox – maybe because of his red hair and beard – that had made the fox come to him and stay?

The more I thought about it the more I was sure the man wouldn't tell me. By now I was in their street, cycling between the crashed cars. They were still strange to me, these cars, even though I'd passed them many times. I'd even tried to draw them, but I couldn't do it. I needed to sit down on the road beside them and draw right there. Either that, or take a couple of photos and try to draw from them. I'd bring my camera next time I came.

The wind was throwing the flames of the bonfire all over the place. I was a bit worried that the van would catch fire, but I said nothing, because the man clearly wasn't worried. He was so close to the fire that at any minute now his beard would catch alight. The fox was nowhere to be seen.

'It's a cold day, Gerard, is it not?'

'Freezing,' I said. 'Where's Russ?'

'He's in the van, under a blanket. He doesn't

like the weather either.'

A sensible creature, I thought to myself. I also decided that this was a good time to slip in the question.

'How did you get Russ?'

'I was wondering when you'd get round to asking that, young man. Well, I'm going to tell you. I got him when he was a cub.'

He stopped there, as if he'd answered my question. I waited, then asked him again.

'*How* did you get him when he was a cub? You still haven't told me.'

'You want to know everything, don't you? I was out for a walk early one morning when I heard a shot. I ran round the corner and saw a farmer neighbour of mine coming up his field with a shotgun in his hand. When he saw me staring at the gun, he said, "That's one fox that's not going to eat any more of my chickens".'

I just smiled at him and walked on, but the truth was I felt sorry for the fox. I've always liked foxes, and I didn't have much time for that farmer. So, after the farmer disappeared, I opened the gate and went into the field. I knew I was trespassing but I didn't think the farmer would shoot me. Besides, for some strange reason, I wanted to see the dead fox. I found him easy enough – and judging by the amount of blood on the ground there wasn't much left in him. Or I should say 'her', as next to the dead fox was a cub, the cutest little thing you ever saw. That was Russ. He was whining away beside his dead mother, so I didn't think twice, I picked him up and took him home.'

'Was your wife with you then?'

'Yes.'

'Did she mind you bringing him back?'

'Not especially. But she didn't pay him much attention, either. And not long afterwards she left. She didn't leave because of Russ, though.'

I hoped he wouldn't get sad again, but he was smiling, remembering.

'I fed him milk from a baby's bottle till he was big enough to eat meat. Then I bought tins of dog-food for him, and got bones in the butcher. Just as if he was a dog. He didn't know any difference. He'd been too young when I

123

found him to remember what it was like to be wild. I am all the life he's known.'

I nodded at that, and thanked him for telling me. It was a nice story – and a better way for them to get together than any I'd imagined. The wind was freezing, though, and I shivered.

'It's too cold to stay here, even with the fire,' I said. 'I'm going home.'

'Wouldn't blame you, at all, Gerard.'

'I'll see you soon,' I said, getting on my bike. As I pedalled away, already thinking of my centrally heated room, I felt a bit guilty, knowing the man couldn't really get in out of the cold – not in the same way anyway.

the dump

On Monday after school I decided I needed to see the man and the fox again, even though I'd been spreading my visits out recently. It was partly because it had been so cold last time, and I felt bad that I hadn't stayed long, and partly because I hadn't seen the fox at all then. I also felt the two of them needed a bit of looking after.

This time it was the man who wasn't there when I arrived. There was no bonfire, the fox was standing at the door of the van, but there was no sign of the man. All my old worries suddenly came back to me.

'Hello,' I said into the van, in case it was his turn to be lying under a blanket there. Knowing his name would be very useful in situations like these, I thought.

There was no reply. I went to the door of the van and looked in. It was a bit of a mess inside, with a very basic bed that hadn't been made, and a battered looking little table by the side of it. There was no room at all to move. I couldn't imagine living in such a cramped space.

Looking around me to make sure the man wasn't approaching I climbed inside. There were a couple of paperbacks on the table, and an old hardback notebook which I picked up and opened. A tattered black and white photograph of a woman fell out – a pretty woman with long black hair. I slipped it back into the beginning of the notebook, opened some pages at random and began to read. Very soon I realised I shouldn't be doing this – it was a very personal diary, and nobody should be reading it but the man.

I decided to get out of the van and go to look for him. He couldn't be far away, could he? I'd never seen the fox and him separated, though. The fox was eyeing me intently. He'd know where the man had gone. It would be useful if he could talk, I thought. I decided to ask him anyway.

'Where has your master gone?'

The little black eyes stared at me, but the fox didn't move.

'Your master, I said. The man, where is he?'

This time the fox turned and walked a bit in the direction of the dump, then stopped and looked back at me. Of course, I thought, the man was in the dump. I should have known that immediately.

I thanked the fox and hurried past him, noticing, though, that he was coming with me. Together we entered the dump. What a varied collection of stuff, I thought. I saw broken television sets, old beds, a rocking-chair, bent bicycle wheels, a golfbag and a lawnmower, a pram with no wheels and a rusty gate. That was only in the early bit, and the dump stretched a good way beyond that. Everything obviously ended up here, sooner or later. If I lived near a dump, I'd make art out of some of the stuff there – lots of the metal things, for example, would be good for sculpture.

Where was the man? Accompanied by the

fox, I carried on deeper into the dump. Beyond it I could hear the crusher doing its business, squashing cars. Every now and again I came across black plastic bags lying amid the other debris. They didn't look very pretty, I thought.

And maybe it was the noise of the crusher, but I started noticing how precarious some of the piles of metal junk were, and how easy it would be for some of them to collapse. Had one fallen on the man, as he rummaged for firewood, and was he lying unconscious under an old fridge? Was he dead, even? Had the fox been on his own all day?

Then, in a lull in the car-crushing, I heard the sound of snapping wood, and saw the man leaning down, breaking off bits of a wardrobe. He had quite a few wooden pieces by his feet.

He straightened up when he saw us.

'Ah, a visitation,' he said. 'Welcome to the dump.'

I nearly told him I'd been worried about him, but I knew he'd laugh it away, so instead I pointed at the wood, and asked him, 'Did you do all that with your bare hands?'

'Cheap wardrobes!' he muttered. 'They're mainly plywood. But they burn OK.'

'It's a pity metal doesn't burn.'

'Oh, there's no shortage of wood dumped here, either, Gerard. It just doesn't stay around long.'

He laughed at that and carried on breaking up the wardrobe.

'What's in the plastic bags?' I asked.

'Don't ask. Often as not it's a dead dog or cat. The stink here, sometimes, in the hot weather . . .'

'Who brings all this stuff here?'

'Cars come at all times, especially at night. Sometimes vans – presumably companies paid to get rid of unwanted things.'

'Does anyone else, except you, come here to take things away?'

'Oh, I see people in here from time to time, picking through the stuff. Why shouldn't they? It's a free country. It's not my dump.'

A fat seagull suddenly landed on a filthy gas cooker and began making its raucous noise.

'Gulls!' said the man, 'I hate them! Horrible

birds! They're not even good to eat! Give me vultures any day.'

'I thought you'd have liked gulls, having been a sailor, and all.'

'Not everything about the sea, I liked.'
He'd dismantled the wardrobe into manageable pieces by now, which – seeing he needed one hand for his black stick – I helped him carry back to the van. Then I watched as he crumpled up pages of newspaper and laid the smaller bits of wood on top before lighting the paper with a match. As the flames grew and the wood started to crackle he added bigger bits of wood. Seeing my interest he grinned.

'There you go, young Gerard. Your first lesson in how to make a fire.'

designing the costume

I took the headmaster's invitation to design my alien costume for the school play very seriously. I wanted it to look different – I didn't want to come out looking like ET's cousin. So I made lots of sketches in my notebook, trying out different ideas. Very quickly I realised that it had to be a practical costume as well as interesting-looking. For example, I was running with the idea of having two heads until I tried to work out how I could speak out of the two heads at once. Speaking out of one only just wouldn't do. I thought about microphones but that seemed far too complicated.

Other ideas were practical enough but unattractive. Resembling a giant slug or beetle, for example. Or a jellyfish. I didn't want to appear on stage looking like any of those.

It was difficult. I could go to the headmaster for help – he'd suggested initially we do it together – but I really wanted to do it myself.

After exploring different shaped heads, none of which looked right, I suddenly remembered what it was I was trying to come up with. It was what a creature from another world might look like. It didn't have to look anything like the creatures of this world – not people, not animals, not insects.

So it wouldn't have to have a head, or legs, or arms. It wouldn't even have to have a voice, although I didn't see how that would work on stage. I could cheat a little bit, I supposed. So I started drawing geometric shapes – squares, rectangles, diamonds, triangles. The triangle looked most promising.

The costume, unlike the drawing, would be three-dimensional – so if I went with the triangle, it would be a cone.

I tried to imagine being inside a cone. It could be a very big cone, so my head would be halfway up and if I spoke it would sound as if I was speaking from my tummy. I could even cut out a mouth there, with weird-looking lips, but no eyes, no nose, no rest of face. Maybe I could even blow bubbles out of the mouth every time I spoke. My voice would have to be very strange, of course. I'd have to think about that.

The more I thought about the cone idea, the more I liked it. The drawings looked good, especially with the bubbles coming from the mouth. I decided the cone should be pale green, and maybe be a bit hairy. It would go right down to the ground, so my feet wouldn't show, and I wouldn't do something as normal, or as earthly, as walking round the stage – no, I'd slither sideways, like you do in socks on polished floorboards. Maybe there were roller-skates with balls instead of wheels which enabled you to go sideways.

These were little practical details that could be sorted out later. I was happy to let the headmaster help with the practical stuff, now that I had come up with the design myself. I couldn't wait to show him.

flu

My dad came home early from work, feeling rotten, and went straight to bed, and next day when I got home from school I was feeling rotten, too. My mum said it was probably flu. She sent me to bed and fussed over the two of us, bringing us hot drinks with stuff in them to make us feel better, and going to the shop to get me lucozade. At my last school I'd always liked being off sick, but I really wanted to be in these days because of the school play. I didn't want to lose my starring role.

So the next morning, despite a headache and a sore throat, and feeling shivery all over, I got dressed and tried to go to school. My mum wasn't having it, at all.

'Are you crazy, Gerard? Get up those stairs and into bed.'

'But Mum, I have the main part in the school play. They're rehearsing this week. I have to be there. If I'm not, someone else will get my part.'

'Don't be silly, no one else will get your part. It might be the most important part but you don't have to say much. You'll easily catch up. And the Head wouldn't let anyone else use your costume, seeing as you designed it.'

It was true, I didn't have many lines to say – and I had them home with me to learn. It was fortunate that I hadn't come down sick before I'd had a chance to show the Head my design. He'd liked it very much, and said he already had ideas on how it could be made. He might even be making it while I was off sick, I thought, and it might be there waiting for me to try out when I got back.

'If you don't stay in bed,' my mother said, 'the flu will get worse. You might end up in hospital, and you certainly wouldn't be able to take part in the play then.'

That did it. I kissed her, went back upstairs, changed my clothes for my pyjamas again, and got back into bed. It did feel better being there.

pinocchio

Four days later I was still at home, and my dad was still with me, although he seemed much better now. He was clearly in no hurry to go back to work. Mum hadn't come down with this flu at all – maybe working in the hospital gave her a kind of immunity.

I was feeling a little better, and I didn't spend all the time in bed. Sometimes I took the duvet downstairs with me and sat on the sofa in front of the big fire my dad had lit. I was surprised by how much attention he was giving me, getting me to talk about school, and the play I was in, and even about the drawing and writing I liked to do – stuff he normally showed no signs of caring about. Maybe it was just the pressure of his work that kept him from having much to do with me normally.

He even asked if he could read me a story. The last time he'd done that was when I was on picture books.

'What story?' I asked.

'A story I loved when I was your age. An Italian story called *Pinocchio.*'

'*Pinocchio*? Like in that cartoon film?'

'The book is much better than the film. Let me read you a bit, and see if you like it. First I'll make a pot of tea.'

I must say, I was surprised by the story. It was about a piece of wood that talked, and when made into a puppet, came to life and was very cheeky and naughty. But the lessons of life – and this living puppet needed a lot of lessons – made him good. It took a long time and many pages, though, for him to learn these lessons, and my dad only got so far before Mum came home and he had to stop to talk to her. It didn't matter. He'd read enough for me to want to finish it on my own, and I had it all read when I went back to school.

It gave me so many ideas, that story, for what I might do in my own writing from now on. I loved the way the writer imagined things, especially what he did with animals – the four black rabbits carrying the little black coffin on their shoulders, the snail that took nine hours to come down from the fourth storey to answer the door, the coach to Playland (where only children lived) pulled by twelve pairs of donkeys, all the same size but a different colour – and all of whom had once been lazy boys who didn't like school. The only thing I didn't like was that one of the most horrible characters in the story was a fox.

And so many strange and unbelievable things happened in the story that it was no problem at all for me to go back to school and imagine I was a cone-shaped alien.

rehearsing

When I finally got back to school the following Monday, I knew all my lines backwards. I'd even practised and worked out the
best way to speak them. I'd say each word twice
in a loud groany whisper. For example one of
my lines was, '*I look into the future and see your
planet dead as Mars.*'

This then became, '*I I look look in in to to the
the fut fut ure ure and and see see your your pla pla
net net dead dead as as Mars Mars.*'

That way I got to speak twice as much, without having to learn any more lines. And it
sounded very creepy. It took a lot of practice,
though, and in rehearsing it on my own at
home I'd decided I had to break up the words
with more than one syllable. The Head
thought that was brilliant. My mum was right –

my staying at home for the first week of rehearsals hadn't harmed me at all. In fact, it had probably helped me, in that I knew exactly how to say my lines at the first rehearsal I attended.

I was a bit disappointed that my costume wasn't ready yet. I asked the Head about it as soon as I saw him, but he said his son, who was an art student, was working on it. He also said it would be worth waiting for. I hoped he was right. Having seen the play in rehearsal I thought it was quite good, but not as surprising.as the story of *Pinnochio*. I definitely had the best part, though.

My favourite line, that I croaked at the President of America (who was played by a girl in my class, a girl I quite liked), was, '*If if you you don't don't zap zap your your miss miss iles iles a a cock cock roach roach will will take take your your place place.*'

I liked the line better when the Head told me what it meant – that cockroaches were the only creatures that would survive a nuclear war, and the only way to avoid one of those was by destroying all our nuclear missiles. I wondered if the audience would understand. When I said the line to my dad he hadn't a clue what I was on about, but he was watching a film on TV at the time.

One other thing I had my character do was breathe very loudly when I wasn't speaking (which was most of the time) – I figured an alien who landed on earth wouldn't be brilliant at breathing, because the air on his planet would be different. I kept the bubble-blowing back until the dress-rehearsal, when I'd be in my costume. I wanted to surprise everybody.

reinforcements

The rehearsals were after school, and I went straight from the third one of these to see the man and the fox. It had to be ten days or more since I'd been to visit them – by far the longest gap in my seeing them since the time I'd clapped eyes on them first. I had had good reason for staying away: the flu, then the rehearsals (they meant I got home from school an hour later than usual, so it was hard to squeeze in time for a visit on top of this) – but I still felt a bit guilty.

When I got to the first crashed car, I was surprised to find the fox standing there on the pavement. He never went anywhere on his own, apart from into the dump, after rats. And the way he was looking at me made me think he was deliberately standing there, waiting for me. Sure enough, he immediately turned around and headed back towards the van. I followed him quickly.

There was no fire, even though it was a particularly cold day. This was a very bad sign. The man had to be inside the van, the door of which was closed. I knocked on the door. A groan came from inside, so I opened the door and looked in. The man was lying in bed with the blankets pulled up to his chin. I could see straight away he didn't look well at all.

I climbed in and went over to him. He smiled at me, with difficulty, and hesitantly took a hand out from under the blankets to touch mine. He felt very warm. He was breathing with difficulty, I noticed – great wheezy breaths, a bit like the ones I was pretending my alien took, only worse. Was it the same flu my dad and I had had? No, he looked sicker than that, I thought.

'What's the matter?' I asked.

At first I thought he wasn't going to answer me, but then he spoke, very weakly and slowly.

'Can't breathe. Hurts me.'

'I'll go for help.' I said. 'I'll be back soon.'

With a last look at him, and at the fox who was now also in the van, I slipped out and ran down the street of crashed cars. It was time my mum got to meet the man and the fox. If anyone could help the man, she could.

hospital

My mum wasted no time in getting the man into hospital. I was there when the ambulance came up and two men loaded him on. Then they went off, with blue lights flashing and sirens wailing.

I wanted to go with them but Mum said I had to look after the fox – that he wouldn't be allowed into a hospital.

'Can I take him home, then?'

'You'd better, Gerard, though I don't know what your father is going to say.'

So I put the fox on the floor of Mum's car and sat on the back seat to keep him company. I opened the window slightly, even though it was cold. She brought us home, came inside for a while, then headed off to the hospital. It was time for her shift but she also said she'd keep looking in on the man.

I was very glad Mum had acted so promply, and that she'd said nothing to me about why I knew the man and the fox so well. No doubt I would get quizzed later, but the fact that she'd allowed me to take the fox home was a good sign. As for the fox – the poor creature didn't know where he was. He probably hadn't been in a house since he'd been a cub and the man had taken him home, and he now just stood there, looking round. I kept stroking him, and whispering that it was all right. I wondered if I should take him up to the bath and shampoo him before my dad got home, but it would be too much of a shock to the fox. Anyway, one of Dad's friends had a dog that stank, and there were never any complaints about that.

I went to the kitchen, got some slices of bacon from the fridge and put them on a plate on the floor. Beside this I left a bowl filled with water, then I called the fox in. He took a bit of persuading, but eventually he did move from where he was standing and came into the kitchen. He needed no persuading to eat and drink.

I was hungry myself, so I made a ham sandwich and gobbled it down. Normally I wouldn't do that before dinner, but Dad would have to cook later and I knew what his cooking was like. We'd get sausages and beans, or maybe a frozen pizza. I wanted to ring my mum to see how the man was doing, but she'd told me once not to ring her at the hospital unless it was an emergency. I didn't know if this was an emergency or not. Maybe now that the man was being looked after by doctors and nurses it was no longer an emergency. I still wanted to know if he was OK.

I heard a key turning in the door, and I ran to see if it was my mum back from the hospital. It was Dad. He put his briefcase down and came into the kitchen, where his eyes lit on the fox.

'What in the name of ...?'

'It's a fox, Dad. He's called Russ. He belongs to a friend of mine who's had to go into hospital.'

My dad just stood there staring at the two of us. I left him like that as I headed for my room, pausing at Russ so he would follow me.

pneumonia

I was awake when my mum came in. I was lying in bed waiting for her, and Russ was lying on the floor nearby. I'd taken him upstairs with me, as he'd looked a bit confused and unhappy since he'd come into the house. I didn't blame him. It was far from what he was used to. And he didn't have his constant companion who'd been with him every day from the time he was a cub.

How was this constant companion doing? This was, of course, why I was waiting up for my mum. Normally I'd have been asleep hours ago but I couldn't think of sleeping till I had a report.

At last I heard the front door open. I went to get out of bed to go down to her, but I heard she was coming up the stairs. She came straight in to me.

'I knew you'd be awake, Gerard, and you'd want to know. Your friend is pretty sick, I'm afraid. He's got pneumonia – double pneumonia. It's as well we got him into hospital.'

'Is pneumonia worse than flu?'

'Yes, Gerard. A lot worse.'

'Will he get better?'

'I think so, I hope so. He's in the best place.'

'Are you getting him special treatment, Mum?'

She laughed at this.

'Everyone who's sick gets special treatment in our hospital. But I've asked the nurses to look after him. You haven't told me how you know him so well.'

'He and the fox used to be sitting in a doorway a few streets away. I told you that when I met them first. I got talking to them, and kept going to see them. We became friends. Then one day they weren't there any more, so I went looking for them. Eventually I found them and would go to visit them sometimes. And the last time I went there I saw the man was sick and went to get you.'

'I should be cross with you, Gerard, but I'm not.'

She leaned down and kissed me on the forehead.

'Go to sleep now.'

'Thanks, Mum. If I go to the hospital after school, will I be allowed to see the man?

'I don't know, Gerard. Depends on how sick he is.'

'Oh please, Mum. I'll just stay a minute.'

'I'll speak to the nurses and see what they say.Goodnight now.'

'Goodnight, Mum.'

As I went to switch my bedside light off, I leaned over and looked down at the fox. He seemed to be asleep. What would I do with him tomorrow? I couldn't take him into school with me. Would he be happy staying here on his own? But that's what dogs had to do, wasn't it? Besides, it was only for a little while. Soon he'd be back with the man.

bubbles

I thought it was going to be hard to concentrate on school and the play rehearsal with all this business involving the man. I was right about school – I was pretty useless in class, and my teacher got stroppy with me a couple of times – but the rehearsal was different. And why was this? Because finally my costume was ready.

It looked just like I'd wanted it to look, even down to the shade of green it was painted. The only thing that was missing was that it wasn't hairy. The Head had told me his son didn't think the hairyness was right. It occurred to me that maybe his son hadn't been able to make it hairy.

I didn't really mind, though. It looked really cool and the mouth in the tummy, with its dark green lips, was very funny. I couldn't wait to get into it. The Head had even managed to get me a pair of those rollerskates I'd been wondering about, the ones that could move sideways. I put them on and the Head lifted the big green cone on top of me. I looked out through the mouth at him and at the rest of the cast, then I got my bubble-maker out of my pocket and sent a stream of bubbles out through the mouth followed by my groany hiss delivering my opening line:

'I I come come to to you you from from a a far far off off pla pla net net.'

There was a gasp from some of the other kids, and the Head clapped his hands and said *'Bravo!'* So I blew out some more bubbles and swivelled round a bit. I was loving this.

One thing I didn't love was that the Head had changed some of the lines in the play, and most of them were my lines! Having learned his original lines so well, it was very hard for me to substitute the new ones. Once I failed three times to say the new line and the Head was getting a little bit annoyed with me, but he noticed he was doing this, and was quick to praise my general performance.

I'd soon get the lines right – if he didn't keep changing them – and I couldn't wait for the actual day of the show. I'd be a star, and my mum and dad would see me.

1 wanted the man to be there as well. I wondered if he would be well enough. I hadn't once spoken to him about the play, as all along I'd hoped I could persuade him to come. If he did come he'd get a surprise to see me like this. He'd know it was me, too, even with the costume and the weird voice. It would cheer him up.

green curtain

I went straight to the hospital after the rehearsal and realised immediately that I had a problem. The hospital was a big place and I didn't know where to find the man. And I couldn't ask what ward he was in, as I didn't know his name.

So I went up to a woman at the front desk and asked for my mother. What I'd have done if my mother hadn't been working her shift then, I didn't know, but fortunately she did.

It took her a while to get to the front desk, but when she did she wasn't surprised to see it was me.

'I'm very busy, Gerard, but I'll quickly take you to your friend. He's in Plunkett Ward, on the fourth floor.'

We went over to the lift and waited with a

male nurse and a woman in a wheelchair. The man and my mum obviously knew each other, but they barely spoke. I was afraid she was going to embarrass me by telling him I was her son. It wasn't that I was embarrassed to be my mum's son, just that I hated being introduced to strangers.

They got out at the third floor and we carried on alone to the fourth. Then Mum took me straight into the ward and up to a nurse who was clearly a friend of hers.

'This is Gerard, my boy, he wants to see the man I had brought in yesterday.'

'Ah, he wants to see Mr Black.'

Mr Black! So that was his name? How did she know this? Had the man told her? Maybe it wasn't his name at all.

'Your friend isn't a well man,' she said. 'He's over here in this bed.'

She indicated a bed that had a green curtain around it and we went behind the curtain. The man was there, and he was awake. He looked sick and still had that wheezing noise when he breathed but he smiled to see me. He didn't seem up to speaking, though.

'As you can see, Mr Black, your young friend has come to visit you.'

The man just kept smiling and looking at me. Even though I was glad to be there I felt very awkward. I hated seeing him here. I made myself speak to him.

'Russ is fine,' I said. 'He's with me.'

The man nodded and smiled some more. This time I smiled back. I wanted to say other things to him but couldn't think what. I was relieved when the nurse said we should let Mr Black rest.

I thanked the nurse and went with my mum to the lift.

'You go back to your work, Mum,' 'I said. I'll let myself out.'

She didn't disagree with this, and as I went down in the lift and walked to the main entrance I thought to myself how I didn't like hospitals – didn't like the smell or the atmosphere, and wondered how my mum could work in one. I hoped the man wouldn't be kept in long. Next time I came I'd bring the fox to cheer him up. I knew I wouldn't be allowed to, and when the fox was discovered I'd be thrown out – but somehow I'd smuggle him in.

the empty bed

I didn't get a chance to fulfil my promise to reunite the man and the fox. After I got home from school the next day, and was about to head off to the hospital with the fox, wearing my big coat, ready to take off and wrap around the fox, my mum came in. She came over straight away and cuddled me, and I knew she had something bad to tell me.

'I'm afraid your friend has gone.'

Gone? I didn't understand her. Had he run away from hospital?

'He's dead, Gerard. He was making progress but he had a relapse early this morning and there was nothing the doctors could do.'

I didn't believe what she was telling me. Hospitals were where people got better. He couldn't be dead.

I struggled away from her, ran to my bike, and was out the door before she could stop me.

'Gerard!' she shouted after me, but I wasn't stopping. I cycled like mad to the hospital, dumped my bike at the front door, and ran to the lift. Come on, come on, come on! I thought, seeing the number stuck on three. Finally it came, and I went up to the fourth floor, and ran into the ward. I went straight over to the man's bed, but it was empty. At that moment the nurse I'd spoken to yesterday came up to me, and Mum came rushing in and led me away.

She put my bike on to the roof-rack and I sat on the front seat beside her, crying. She had one hand on the wheel and one on my neck. Neither of us spoke.

When I got home I went straight up to my room and held the fox. Something about the way he felt in my arms today made me believe he knew the man was dead.

the sad star

I didn't go to the man's funeral. Nobody told me where or when it was taking place. I wanted to pull out of the play, but my mum wouldn't let me. She said the man would have wanted me to go ahead and play the part well. I'd told her about all his stories of his travels and his early life, and about my showing him the drawings I'd done. I kept doing new drawings of the man which I left lying around the house. My dad didn't understand the way I felt about the man, and he kept muttering about the fox, about the smell in the house, and the way the creature kept staring at him, but he saw I was upset and didn't say too much.

Dad would have to get used to the fox, as he was officially mine now. My mum had brought home a piece of paper, witnessed by two nurses, which she said was the man's last will and testament. In it, he left me the fox and his collection. He signed it James Black (aka The Man with the Fox).

So I had to look after the fox, as best I could. The collection I could live without, but I did go round to the van with my mum and the fox one day, and took away the small collection of car stuff. I left the other bigger things. I also took the man's diary, with the woman's photograph in it. One day, when I felt the time was right, I'd read it. Now that he was dead it would be OK to do that.

And I did perform in the play. I was still sad, but I kept thinking of the man throughout, and my sadness helped me play the part well – it made my warnings about what people were doing to their planet sound even more gloomy and serious. It did occur to me as I played the part, though, that I should be including in my warnings the way people ignored the homeless. The Head was very pleased with my performance, as were my parents – I'd never seen Dad so happy with me – and even the other kids seemed to be proud of me.

And when my parents took me to Pizza Express afterwards, and I had my favourite Americana, with pepperoni on it, I almost stopped being sad.

paris

There was a better treat in store for me. My dad announced we were going to Paris for Christmas. *Us* going somewhere – and somewhere as interesting as Paris?? What had happened?

Dad said his new job was going well, and we all needed a little break. He also said he hated the whole business of Christmas – extended families and turkeys and all the rest – and by going to Paris we'd escape it all. I quite liked Christmas, and I didn't see how, by going to Paris, we'd escape it – it would still be Christmas in Paris – but I wasn't going to argue with him.

My Mum was winking at me. She'd obviously had something to do with this surprising decision, and indeed I remembered

complaining to her that we never went anywhere, to which she'd replied that maybe we
would. Well, now we were. I got a bit sad again
when I remembered that it was hearing about
the man's travels that had made me want to
travel. Had he ever been to Paris? It wasn't one
of the places he'd mentioned, but he'd also said
there was no place he hadn't been to.

What would we do with the fox when we
were in Paris? We were going for a week, my
dad had said, and I knew you weren't allowed
to take animals abroad – well, you could, but
they had to stay in quarantine, because of rabies
fears. Even if we were allowed, I couldn't see
my Dad agreeing to take the fox, or the hotel in
Paris agreeing, either. I asked Mum what would
happen and she said there were places you
could leave animals to be looked after while
you were abroad, and that's what we would do.
You had to pay for it, she said, but not too
much.

So we flew to Paris for a week and I loved it.
It was the first time I'd been in an aeroplane
and I found it very exciting – I wanted to get

out and roll around on the clouds. I couldn't understand why my dad was nervous.

We did a lot of walking in Paris, especially by the River Seine. We also visited museums and galleries – I loved seeing all the paintings – and went to Mass in the Cathedral of Notre Dame. We went up the Eiffel Tower, and took the train out to the Palace of Versailles. And we ate in loads of restaurants. My mum especially liked that part.

It was a lovely holiday, but I was pleased to get home. First thing the next morning my mum and I went to collect the fox. He was glad to see me and I was glad to see him.

the boy with the fox

Over the next few months I got to know the fox very well and began to feel I was as close to him as the man had been. I knew the man would have wanted that. I took him everywhere with me. I had the pannier on my bike moved from the back to the front, so the fox could sit there and look ahead when I rode about – it was my equivalent of sitting there with the fox round my neck.

At weekends, especially when the weather was good, I was out with the fox as much as I could. People began to recognise us, and wave to us, and I would hear some refer to me as the boy with the fox. I liked that. I took him to visit the One-Legged Englishman, and into the park to introduce him to Annie May. Having the fox made me very popular with other kids who all wanted to stroke him. Sometimes I'd be asked to join in football matches in the park, and the fox would run around after the ball, too, and the boys would love this. The fox was initially a bit surprised by all the attention, and would act shy, but he soon got used to being popular. He never got over his old ways completely, though – several times in the park he pounced on squirrels or pigeons and proceeded to eat them. This disgusted some of the girls, in particular, but the fox didn't remain unpopular for long.

I got accustomed to the two of us being photographed by tourists, and once my mum pointed out to me that we were in the newspaper. She cut out the photograph and framed it. My Mum became quite fond of the fox, and sometimes took him for walks herself. I think she enjoyed attracting the stares. Even my dad got used to the fox being about, though I couldn't exactly say they became friends.

And often, as I was out with the fox, and people were stopping to look at us, I thought of the man, and all the places he'd travelled to before he'd met the fox, and I promised myself

I'd take the fox to some of those places, one day when borders and quarantine were done away with, and no one anywhere was homeless.

the simon community

The Simon Community was founded by the late Anton Wallich-Clifford back in sixties London. He was a probation officer, first becoming interested in the problems of the homeless when, as a child, his mother insisted that he carry a few pence in his pocket to give to the poor.

The name Simon came from Simon of Cyrene, the unknown citizen who assisted Christ to carry his Cross. 'That's all we're attempting to do,' said Wallich-Clifford, who brought the Simon Community to Ireland in 1969. 'We can't carry the individual cross of every man and woman, but we can be there to put a shoulder under that cross.' Emphasising that Simon deals with men and women of all faiths and none, and their workers are likewise.

Wallich-Clifford added that 'in trying to follow Simon we are, in fact, following a way of the cross and, in a way, personally living out the Gospel message.'

Simon people are those on the very bottom rung of the ladder. People who cannot adjust to the world around them, for a variety of reasons. It can be addiction (overwhelmingly alcohol), or abuse, or family circumstances. They cannot cope with life, yet all need love, acceptance and care, which Simon aims to provide. Simon People come from all walks of life – you meet the doctor, the engineer, the policeman, the nurse, and the man of the cloth. The dividing line between 'them' and 'us' can be very fine indeed.

'The problem is increasing, it's getting bigger', said Anton Wallich-Clifford, almost thirty years ago. Sadly, those words are ever more relevant and necessary today. We can only hope that the vision of the group he founded will continue to inspire and motivate the like-minded people who make up the Simon Community.

'I firmly believe we have to establish a truly caring community if we are in fact to be worthy of ourselves as human beings. We cannot neglect our brother, we are our brother's keeper. It is not enough to say "the State takes cares of this, I don't have to bother". I think it is very important that each and every one of us, no matter what our age, no matter what our background, no matter what our condition, should be concerned about the guy next door, about the person who's sleeping out, the homeless and the rootless.'

John Walshe